MONTANA MISTLETOE

ALSO BY KIM LAW

The Wildes of Birch Bay

Montana Cherries

Montana Rescue

Montana Mornings

Montana Mistletoe

Montana Dreams

Montana Promises

Montana Homecoming

Montana Ever After

Turtle Island Novels

Ex on the Beach

Hot Buttered Yum Two

Turtle Island Doves (novella)

On the Rocks

Sugar Springs Novels

Sugar Springs

Sweet Nothings

Sprinkles on Top

The Davenports

Caught on Camera

Caught in the Act

Caught off Guard

Deep in the Heart

Hardheaded

Softhearted

Holly Hills

"Marry Me, Cowboy" (novella), Cowboys for Christmas

Montana

MISTLETOE

Kim Law

J-KO PUBLISHING

Published by J-Ko Publishing

ISBN: 978-1950908035

To Kimberly Dawn and Lizzie Shane – Friendship, brainstorming, reading, editing, encouragement, panic-alleviating . . . you've both done it all for this one, and I am immensely and forever grateful. I honestly can't say thank you enough.

CHAPTER ONE

"I'm going to have a new momma."

Bree Yarbrough heard the softly murmured words spoken at her side, but she didn't pull her gaze from the couple standing face-to-face, twenty feet in front of her hometown's high school football bleachers. Her heart pounded as she watched. Her oldest sister and the man she hadn't seen or spoken with in several weeks had finally quit kissing, yet they remained where they'd rushed to each other after the game. Gabe stood on one side of the chain-link fence, Erica on the other, and their foreheads were now tilted together. Wide smiles plastered their faces.

"One more, Coach." Someone from behind Bree egged them on. "You can't stop now. I'm taking notes on how it's done."

Bree grinned at the teasing and glanced around at the happiness greeting her from all corners of the stands. She blinked at the tears threatening in her eyes. Love had won. And everyone there knew it.

"They are going to get married, right?" The girl spoke at her side again, the words as soft as before, and Bree looked down at the seven-year-old who waited anxiously for an answer. "That's what the kissing means, right?" Jenna persisted. "That Miss Erica loves my daddy now?"

Bree nodded, her heart growing for the child she'd only recently met. "That's definitely what the kissing means. But we'll have to wait and see if they're going to get married or not. We can only keep our fingers crossed and hope." She did know that her sister *wanted* to marry Gabe. That's why they'd cut their road trip short and shown up where they knew Gabe would be tonight.

"Well, if he *doesn't* marry her"— Gabe's father spoke from her other side—"I'll be having a long talk with my oldest son, I can tell you that. This isn't one to let slip away again."

All attending Wilde family members nodded in agreement and began gathering their things for the long drive back to Birch Bay, and with sighs of longing whispering throughout the stands, the crowd finally began to disperse. Bree scooped up the blanket she'd snagged from her car as she'd hurried into the game and glanced around for her own family. Then she began weaving her way toward them.

"Hey, pipsqueak." She bent to hug her youngest nephew when she reached them and faked a grunt as Ethan, the older sibling, rammed into her legs.

"You should have sat with *us*," five-year-old Ethan complained. "Were you over there rooting for *them*?"

"Rooting for the other team?" Bree rounded her eyes in horror as she raised her hands in surrender. "Are you kidding me?" Her hometown took football seriously, and *nothing* was more serious than the Montana high school state championship. "I was for Silver Creek all the way."

At least, for *most* of the way. Because she couldn't say she'd have been *too* upset if Birch Bay, led by Erica's beau Gabe—and Gabe's oh-so-yummy brother Cord—had taken the win on this one.

"Then you should have sat with *us*." Ethan refused to relent.

2

"You're right." She gave him a knowing nod before shooting a quick glance to the other side of the field. The team benches now sat empty. "I probably should have sat with you." Her gaze roamed toward the concrete building housing the locker rooms, seeking out a tall, dark-haired former high school football champion, himself. All she caught sight of, though, was her sister and Gabe walking hand in hand. She brought her gaze back to her nephews. "But isn't the more important issue at the moment the fact that your Aunt Erica is currently walking away with the *coach* of that very team?" She pointed to the evidence. "Don't you think we should go rescue her before he tries to smuggle her away from here on the team bus?"

And maybe they'd catch sight of another Wilde while at it? Before *he* disappeared from town as well.

The three-year-old giggled at her words, while Ethan rolled his eyes as if to indicate she hadn't changed the subject off her seeming disloyalty as cleverly as she'd hoped.

"Aunt Bree is right," her mother said. She gathered up the pile of blankets the chilly night had called for. "Bree and Erica are in town at the same time for once, and Annalise will be arriving tomorrow as well. So, we're having a long-awaited family dinner tomorrow night. And that means we can't let Aunt Erica slip away."

Ethan looked up at his grandmother. "Daddy said it'll be kind of like Thanksgiving, but not."

"Your dad is exactly right." Her mom began herding them all down the bleachers. "Aunt Annalise and you boys and your mama and daddy won't be here *on* Thanksgiving this year, so we're having it a little early. But I might cook another turkey on the actual day of Thanksgiving if either of your other aunts stick around."

Her mom shot Bree a look, but Bree ignored the message behind it.

Stay home for once, will you?

And she ignored it because she happened to know that *for once*, she might just *be* staying home. At least through Christmas. Only, she hadn't informed her parents of that yet.

And she hadn't informed her parents because in the back of her mind, she wanted to leave herself an out. Just in case she changed her mind at the last minute.

She'd be an idiot to change her mind, though. She knew that. This was the type of opportunity budding artists didn't pass up. Staying would mean working alongside Mrs. Cory to create a one-of-a-kind mural inside the town's newly renovated office complex. A mural that, with Beverly Cory's name attached, would receive attention. Which meant that *she* would receive attention. And a little attention could go a long way in the art world.

She had a meeting scheduled with both Mrs. Cory and the mayor of Silver Creek on Monday morning to sign the contract and discuss the final design.

Unless, of course, she decided not to do it.

"You are staying at the house tonight, correct?" Her mother's look was back again, and Bree barely contained an eye roll.

"That's the plan, Mother. Like I told you over the phone."

"Good." Her mom gave a decisive nod—as if *her* words had been the deciding factor in Bree's decision—and as they headed through the gate exiting the field, her dad moved to her side and slipped an arm around her shoulders.

"We've missed you," he whispered and followed it up with a wink.

She rested her head against his shoulder and sighed. "And I've missed you. I've missed *home*."

Her dad gave her a squeeze.

It had been several months since she'd been home, and then only for a couple of days. And that had been her norm since graduating high school. But truth be told, Montana was home, and it always would be. It's where her heart was drawn to and where she hoped to one day return permanently.

She just wasn't sure Silver Creek would be where she would return to.

"There's Aunt Ewica!" Ian, the younger of the two, shouted as he pointed toward the school bus in the parking lot. He bounced on his toes. "I miss Ewica. I haven't seen her in *fowever*."

He hadn't seen Erica since she'd moved to Birch Bay three months before.

"Then run give her a hug," Bree's mother encouraged.

Ian looked up with eyes full of excitement, and then he and Ethan took off as one, both barreling toward the bus currently being loaded with slump-shouldered football players who'd come darned close to taking the championship.

Erica looked away from Gabe as if sensing the incoming tumble of arms and legs and laughed out loud as the boys plowed into her. Bree watched, her own smile on her face, as her oldest sister and her only nephews greeted each other. Her heart felt fuller tonight, and she wasn't sure if it was the fact that Erica had made up with the man she hoped to spend the rest of her life with or if it was because *she* was back home and intended to stick around for a while.

She caught sight of Gabe's brother coming around the back of the bus, his dark head bent in concentration and both hands seeming to be searching his jeans' pockets, and she had the thought that there was one more way she could make her heart fuller still. Or, at least, a *part* of her would be fuller.

A giggle caught in the back of her throat at the thought. Did she dare?

Did she want to?

Deep down, wasn't that what she'd hoped might happen when she'd texted him they'd be at the game tonight?

She looked down at the ground, not ready to make eye contact if Cord happened to look her way. Since their brief meeting in Birch Bay two months before, they'd been texting on and off. Just as friends, mostly. But recently . . . those texts had taken a decided turn from friendly to *more*. And she was *so* ready to see what more felt like.

Another giggle bubbled up, this one escaping as she blew out a deep breath, and she pressed a hand to her mouth to try to contain it. Because yes, as crazy as the idea was, she wanted to do this.

But where? And when?

Her palms began to itch. Was this the type of thing she could actually make happen tonight?

Cord didn't live anywhere near Silver Creek—nor even Birch Bay. He lived hours from both cities and had been helping out with the team only as a favor to his brother. Which meant, if not tonight, then when?

She licked her suddenly parched lips. If not tonight, then she might lose her nerve.

Looking back, she realized that Cord no longer stood by the bus. He'd walked away and was heading to the locker room building. She glanced back to Erica, intent on telling her sister to catch a ride home with their parents, but Erica was the one now giving her "the look."

"No," Erica said, the word bitingly clear, even across the distance.

"No, what?" their mother chimed in.

Gabe even looked up from whomever he'd been speaking with, as if to see what had Erica practically shouting.

Bree gave her sister a hard stare, her eyes silently begging her to say nothing more, then turned and flashed her mom a smile. "Will you give Erica a ride home tonight, Mom?" She peered to the other side of their mother. "You have room in the car, right, Dad?"

"Of course we have room," her dad replied.

Puzzlement crossed their mother's face as she once again

glanced in the direction of Erica, and Bree sensed that her sister was heading their way. "But where are *you* going?" Her mother turned back. "You said you were staying at the house."

"And I *will* stay at the house." Bree captured her mother's hands and rushed to finish. "I promise. I'll even stay until Christmas." She brightened her smile. "How about that?"

"What?" Both her parents spoke at the same time.

"Until Christmas?" Surprise slackened her mother's jaw.

"Yes." Bree silently cursed the impulse that made her blurt that out. "But I might be late tonight, that's all. I saw someone I want to say hi to." She motioned back toward the empty stands as half the stadium lights above them went out. "We might hang out a while. You know . . . catch up a little."

Her mother's features once again shifted. "Are you talking about—"

"Excuse us, Mother." Erica's words bit into their conversation at the same time the tips of her fingers dug into Bree's upper arm. "I need to talk to my sister. *Alone.*"

Erica dragged Bree off to the side without giving their parents a chance to protest, but instead of turning to face her busybody sister, Bree trained her gaze on the now-closing door that led to the locker rooms for both teams. Cord had just slipped inside.

"Whatever thoughts are going through your head"—Erica gritted the words out, pulling Bree in closer as she spoke—"stop them right now."

When Bree didn't respond, Erica shook her arm.

"We've had this discussion, Bree," she hissed out. "He's ten years older than you. He's been with all kinds of women."

Bree finally quit ignoring the glare of her sister's gaze and brought her own around to meet it. "And maybe *I've* been with all kinds of *men.*"

"Yes,"—Erica paused, her lips turning down at the corners—"maybe you have. And I know that's your business and not mine. But Bree," she whispered, "I just don't want to see you hurt.

And *no*, before you ask, I *don't* think Cord would hurt you intentionally. If I did, I'd have a talk with him myself. I'd have *Gabe* talk to him. But, honey"—she squeezed Bree's hand, her eyes imploring now—"you're too young. You don't—"

Bree covered her sister's mouth, stopping the flow of words. They'd had this conversation more than once in the last week. Ever since she'd admitted that she and Cord had been texting. And no matter what Erica said, it wasn't going to change Bree's mind.

Yes, he was ten years older.

And yes, he'd no doubt been with all sorts of women. He was a *total* catch, and she knew he liked to play. So what? That only meant he had experience.

Why couldn't she play, too?

Why couldn't she gain experience?

It wasn't like she was looking for love and commitment. *Geez.* She knew she was too young for that. She wasn't even looking for anything beyond tonight.

But being back here in Silver Creek . . . and ignoring thoughts of what happened the night before she'd left . . . All of that made her *want* to get lost in someone else for a night.

It made her want to *be* someone else.

And anyway, wasn't it time she did this?

She slowly lowered her fingers from Erica's mouth. "He is not going to break my heart, if that's what has you so worried." She didn't take her eyes off her sister's. "And I promise to keep it light. Whatever happens will *not* affect how we behave whenever we both have to be at yours and Gabe's wedding."

The mention of Erica's biggest hope softened her eyes a fraction.

"But Erica . . ." Bree looked toward the concrete building once again, and she replayed the last few minutes of the night of her eighteenth birthday. She needed a new memory associated with

Silver Creek to get her through the next six weeks. Even if the star player of her old memory no longer lived in this town.

She closed her eyes so her sister couldn't read the truth inside her then reopened them once she had herself under control.

"I know what I'm doing." She squeezed her sister's fingers, same as Erica had done to her, and let the confidence she'd spent the last three years honing shine through. "So, go home with Mom and Dad. And do *not* wait up for me."

Erica's lips parted, but Bree continued before she could speak.

"Or I swear on our grandmother's Montana State beauty crown, if you give me so much as one more second of grief about this,"—she narrowed her eyes, a spark burning inside them—"the first thing I'll do when I get home tomorrow morning is tie you to a chair and force you to listen to *all* the dirty details of *everything* we do tonight."

The words snapped Erica's mouth shut. She stared wordlessly for a few seconds, then let out a dry, humorless chuckle. "*Fine.* I'll shut up and let you do you. But please"—she pulled Bree in for a tight hug—"promise me that you'll be careful."

Bree turned her mouth to her sister's ear. "I'm always careful."

CHAPTER TWO

The truth was, she really *was* always careful. Not that most people believed that—nor had she given them reason to. She'd ignored her parents' wishes for college and hightailed it out of town practically the minute she'd turned eighteen. Since then, she'd routinely bounced from city to city or even continent to continent, whichever struck her fancy or caught her attention next. And she often took random jobs—no matter how odd—to support her travels and her art supplies. But as free-spirited as she may be, she never "jumped" when it was something that might hurt her on a more personal level. Been there, done that.

Would be more than a few years before considering it again.

And sitting atop the visiting team's office desk now, her coat and jeans tossed over the back of a chair and her unbuttoned blouse showcasing generous cleavage, a flat stomach, and a naughty hint of her pale-pink panties, posed no threat of hurting her in any fashion. She'd seen Cord exit another door of the building as she'd been coming in, so she'd hurried to find the perfect location and had texted him to come back. She knew what she *was* and what she was *not* getting into. And Cord Wilde, the uber sexy doctor who liked to change up women as often as he changed lab coats, did *not* pose a threat to her psyche.

The man who showed up at the office door just now, however?

Did.

"Justin!" Bree screeched and reached for her blouse, knocking over a cup of pencils in her haste. She'd have sworn the building was empty.

"Bree?" The man who'd once been her best friend—as well as her biggest crush—gawked at her. Once recognition settled, though, his look went from shock to flatlining. His eyes traveled over her. "Well, isn't this a familiar scene."

Fury sliced through her. "It's a scene that is *not* for you." She pointed with her free hand. "Get out."

Instead of doing as she commanded, however, the man had the audacity to step into the room. "I don't think so." He bypassed a runaway pencil, eyed the rolling desk chair that held the majority of her clothes, then leaned back against the wall directly in front of her. "I mean . . . a guy walks into a room and finds a girl half dressed like this . . ."

He shrugged instead of finishing his sentence, his gaze remaining passive, and fire erupted inside her.

"I'm warning you, Justin Cory." *Damn it*, why had she thought this was a good idea? She clutched harder at her shirt. "Get. *Out!*"

She jabbed a finger toward the door again. The blasted man had had his chance.

And anyway, what was he doing here?

"Bree?" Her name came from Cord that time, his voice, as well as his footsteps, echoing through the empty hallway. She opened her mouth, her gaze going from the open doorway back to Justin, as horror filled her.

Justin remained unaffected.

"I got your text," Cord continued. She heard the jangle of his keys. "I came in looking for my keys earlier, but I found them already," he called out before his tone became teasing. "But if there's something *else* I should . . ."

His words died out as he appeared in the doorway and caught sight of her sitting practically naked on the scratched laminate.

Then he took in Justin.

"Oh." Cord's mouth formed a perfect O with the word, and Bree closed her eyes.

Christ almighty, this was *not* how she'd seen this going.

"I take it I'm interrupting something," Cord began, *"unless"*— she peeked back out at his pause, and he lifted his chin, his eyes taking on a look she couldn't decipher—"you texted *both* of us to meet you here?"

Cord's meaning rang clear.

"No!" Her eyes went wide. Of course she hadn't texted both of them! She didn't want a threesome!

What a spectacular mess.

"I only texted *you*." She flapped a hand at Justin. *"He* wasn't invited."

"Yet, here he is." Justin's words were spoken softly, and he hadn't moved from his reclined position. Nor had he allowed any emotion to register on his face.

The air in the room suddenly felt chillier, and she wished she were wearing her clothes.

She tugged at the material of her blouse until the sides overlapped.

"I think maybe I should go." Cord made the statement, but he didn't move to leave. Instead, he turned his full attention on Bree. "If everything is all right here?"

Of course everything wasn't all right here! The wrong man had shown up for her seduction!

She couldn't manage any words, though. Shame had too tight a hold on her.

"Bree?" Cord said the word carefully, as if inching out onto a pond he wasn't certain had frozen over yet, and this time she

managed to shake her head. She lowered her gaze so she didn't have to look at either of them.

"It's okay." Justin spoke when it became obvious she had no plans to. "Bree and I go way back."

Bree continued staring at the floor.

"In what way?" The tone in Cord's question had Bree closing her eyes once again. Cord might be a flirt—and *exceptional* at it when he wanted to be—but she'd seen his true colors the night she'd met him. He liked women, yes. And he slept with a lot of them. But he did *not* get involved if they didn't know the score, which also meant he did his best not to hurt them.

Apparently, that white knight part of him didn't allow him to walk away from a situation if he thought someone *else* might do the hurting, either. He was asking if Bree would be safe left alone with Justin.

"He's fine," Bree finally croaked out. She stared at the scuffed toes of Cord's cowboy boots. "He won't take advantage of me. He was a friend once. We lived next door to each other."

Still, Cord didn't move. "Friends can change."

She shook her head again. "He hasn't. Trust me."

He didn't want her then . . .

He wouldn't want her now.

After another impenetrable moment of silence, Cord stepped forward and lifted her chin. She sensed Justin stiffening at the contact, but he didn't move from the wall.

"Text me later tonight?" Cord said.

She nodded mutely. He wasn't asking to hook up with her later. She had a feeling any chance of that had just fallen through. He only wanted to make sure she made it home okay.

CHAPTER THREE

The thin layer of dust disappeared under the swipe of the cloth as Justin worked his way down the upper trim of his mother's kitchen cabinets. When he reached the end, he shook out the rag, letting the collected particles fall to the waiting trash can below, then reversed his path for a second pass. He could hear his mother rummaging around in the family room down the hall, and the sense of rightness he'd felt when he'd first arrived home two weeks before once again settled over him. He hadn't been around this time of year since going away for his under-graduate degree, so he'd missed the annual pre-Thanksgiving "spring" cleaning. It felt right to be able to help again, though. And he was glad to be home permanently. Glad he'd be able to do this for his mom every year.

He stepped back from the section he'd just finished, flicked his hand at a puff of dust that had fallen to the quartz countertop, and moved to the other side of the room. As he started on that set of cabinets, however, his gaze wandered through the window above the kitchen sink. And landed squarely on Bree Yarbrough.

The muscles in his shoulders tensed.

He hadn't stuck around the night before. He'd had no desire

to hear anything she might come up with to explain herself. Instead, as the other man's footsteps had echoed down the hallway, he'd silently counted to five, and then *he'd* left. Only, he'd gone in the opposite direction.

But now he wished he *had* stuck around.

Now he wanted to ask her what the fuck? Was that the way she went after *every* man she wanted?

And how often had it gotten the results she sought?

Irritation had him grinding his teeth as he watched her. She'd come out to her parents' front porch swing with her oldest sister, the light above them shining in the growing darkness, and he couldn't miss the animation illuminating her face as she talked. She'd always been like that. Excited about whatever it was she had on her mind. Willing to go after anything and everything she wanted.

"That spot is clean enough, Justin."

He jerked at the sound of his mother's voice, then realized he'd been moving his hand in a repeating circle over the front of the cabinet door. "Oh." He dipped his chin, horrified at the feeling of heat climbing his neck. This wasn't the first time his mother had caught him sneaking peeks at the house next door.

"What has you so interested out there?"

"Nothing," he mumbled. He went back to wiping down the cabinets.

His mother didn't let that pass for an answer, of course. Instead, she crossed the room, her wheelchair motor humming softly as she closed in and inched under the lowered kitchen sink. She shifted a stack of magazines to the countertop, then leaned forward and peered through the window. *"Ah."*

He closed his eyes briefly.

"Ah, nothing, Mother." He silently begged her to say no more. "It's just that I haven't . . . *seen* her for a while."

Not with clothes on, anyway.

He rolled his shoulders to ease the tightness in his neck as his mother dumped the magazines in the recycling bin. And he prayed they could get back to work. *Silently.*

That wasn't to be, though. "You need to talk to her."

He kept his tone calm. "I don't ne—"

"She's home for several weeks this time."

That brought his gaze back to hers. Bree was home for more than just a drive-by?

Well, wasn't that big of her?

The corners of his mouth pulled down as he thought about the years of friendship they'd once shared, even with the gap of years between them. At how that friendship had only grown, no matter that he'd often been away at college.

Then he thought about the summer before he'd started grad school. The night of Bree's eighteenth birthday.

He swallowed against a suddenly dry throat. Bree had been home several times since that night, and for some of those times, he'd also been in Silver Creek—between semesters of grad school, for a couple of weeks before he'd started his physical therapy internship—but to hear his mother tell it, she'd never stuck around for more than a couple of days.

And *they'd* never so much as said boo to each other again.

And damn it, that pissed him off. He'd done nothing wrong that night.

Yes, he'd hurt her. He knew that. And he hated that. But he hadn't *meant* to hurt her. And he still wouldn't apologize for it.

He ground his teeth together once again. A guy should be applauded for exhibiting the control he had. Not condemned.

His mother hadn't said anything else as he'd dipped into the past. She'd only waited patiently, her expression saying that it was his turn to talk. So, he finally shook his head.

"It doesn't matter how long she's home for, Mom. Trust me. There's nothing to talk about. It's been three and a half years, and I'm sure she's fine. Just as *I'm* fine," he finished in a grumble.

Of course, he'd have been *more* fine if he hadn't walked in on that little scene last night.

He turned away, not wanting his mother to see the annoyance threatening to return. When Cord Wilde had shown up the night before . . . when he'd put his hand under Bree's chin and lifted her eyes to his. . .

His mother circled him, not letting him escape the moment, and captured his hands with hers. And as complete and total love stared up at him, he couldn't help but think that for someone who had a million reasons to hate her only son, she'd always done an exceptional job at doing just the opposite.

"I *need* you to talk to her," she stressed, and this time her tone was more pleading than commanding. "Because I know *why* she's home. And I worry that once she finds out that the project I asked her to come home to help me with is being done in the same office complex where you work . . ."

His shoulders slumped as understanding dawned. "You asked her to help you with the mural project?"

"I did."

"But . . . *why?*" His mother was a world-renowned artist. Her name on the piece—on *any* piece—was everything. "I thought you had interns lined up to do the transfer." Murals weren't her typical medium, what with the inability of being able to work from scaffolding while in her wheelchair, but that's what the interns were for. They'd replicate her vision from intricately drawn grids to the wall.

It would still be her piece. Her artistry.

"I don't understand," he went on. "You don't need anyone to—"

She squeezed his hands in hers. "I don't need anyone, *no*. But, honey, I *want* her to do this." She nodded, and excitement lit her eyes. "I want what she does—what she'd already begun to excel at before she left here—to be showcased on the wall. I want it to be a masterpiece."

"It *will* be a masterpiece." He'd seen the design she'd already gotten pre-approval on.

"But I want it to be *her* masterpiece, Justin."

The declaration stopped him, and he released his mom's hands. She'd always had a soft spot for Bree. Practically since the moment they and his father had first moved to town. And Bree *did* have talent. At least, she once had. She'd been exploding with it. He hadn't kept up with her since heading off to graduate school, however, so he didn't know how far she'd taken it.

"I need you to clear the air with her, Justin. This is important to me. We meet to sign the contract on Monday, and I can't have her running again just because you're home."

"But she didn't run because of me the first time. And you know that. She was always planning to go." Hell, his mother had encouraged it. Upon graduation, Bree planned to travel the world. To go where the wind took her. *Grow* as an artist from seeing the great works up close.

"But I also know that she'd always planned to come home," she said softly, and the air in his chest leaked out of him.

"She *does* come home, Mother." He motioned toward the window to make his point, but his mom didn't say anything else. And once again, just like on that night and so many that had come after it, guilt drenched him.

He paced to the other side of the room, considering his mother's request, and stopped only when the back door allowed no additional distance to be put between them. Then he stared out at the garage apartment he'd so recently moved into. If Bree planned to be home for several weeks, they'd most likely be living within feet of each other. Which he would be fine with. He could stay out of her way, and he had no doubt she'd stay out of his.

But then he thought about their years of friendship. About the first day she'd laid eyes on him and had made it her mission to "take him under her wing."

A faint smile passed over his mouth. She'd been only thirteen at the time, while he'd been on his way to eighteen, but that hadn't stopped the force that was his new neighbor. Bree had taken one look at him and recognized his skill of staying in the shadows—particularly when tossed into new situations—and had demanded he drive her into town so she could "introduce him around."

Bree was an extrovert from the inside out. She loved people and events. He was the complete opposite. Yet somehow, even with the age difference, that combination had worked for them. From the outside looking in, they'd had nothing in common, yet over the years, whenever he'd been home from school, they'd continually migrated toward each other. Whenever they had news to share . . . When troubles had them seeking an ear in which to talk things out . . .

Simply put, their friendship had been real. And he'd *valued* that relationship.

And darn it, he'd missed it these last three years!

He glanced to the backyard of the house next door. He couldn't see the house itself, but he could "see" Bree sitting in the swing at the back of their property. He could imagine his friend waving him over, urgently wanting to share her latest drawing or sculpture.

And he could hear her telling him that she loved him. That she'd move to Bozeman to be with him when he went to grad school.

He hung his head. He had done the right thing.

"She won't want to talk to me, Mom." He turned as he spoke, certain in his statement. After last night, he suspected Bree would be fine never laying eyes on him again.

"But she *needs* to talk to you, honey. Whatever she took away from that night—"

"Mom. Stop." He held up his hands as if to ward her off. His mother knew way too much of what had gone on between him and Bree. She didn't know all of it, of course. She didn't know that he'd given Bree her first kiss exactly two years *before* the night in question—on her sweet sixteen, no less. Or that she'd purposely saved herself for him. That she'd believed just because she'd turned eighteen that their age difference no longer mattered. As if age difference had been the only thing keeping them from being together.

But his mother *did* know that Bree had been in his bedroom that night. That things hadn't ended well.

And she knew that Bree had left town unexpectedly the next morning.

"Just go over and say hi," she suggested. "Let her know you're home. That you can still be friends."

He let out a dry chuckle, and his mother tilted her head.

"You don't want to be friends with her?" she asked.

"I'd be fine being friends." He just didn't expect it to ever happen.

He looked toward the window over the sink again and saw that Bree and Erica were now greeting their brother and his family along with Annalise and her boyfriend. Phillip and Ellen Yarbrough had come outside, as well. And then he pictured his one-time friend working alongside his mother to create the mural the town had commissioned and planned to unveil as part of the annual Christmas Eve festivities.

He wanted Bree to have that opportunity.

And truth be told, he'd love seeing how far she'd grown as an artist.

He'd also just love seeing—*and talking*—to her again.

"Fine." He shot an annoyed look at his mother. "I'll *try*. But I have to warn—"

"Beverly?" his father's voice cut off his own.

"In the kitchen."

Justin didn't mutter another word as he watched his mom immediately change modes. She patted at her hair as if to make sure all was in place, and he realized for the first time that she'd changed clothes while she'd been out of the room earlier. She'd also spritzed on a fair amount of her favorite perfume.

"Your dad's taking me out to dinner," she explained, her eyes brightening the closer his dad's footsteps got. "At that new steak-house that just opened in town. We heard it's very romantic," she whispered.

"Yeah?" He eyed the opening to the kitchen as he spoke, all thoughts of Bree and "clearing the air" forgotten. His parents' relationship had always astounded him. "You'll have to let me know how it is."

"I will. But don't plan on hearing about it until *tomorrow.*"

She laughed at her not-so-subtle "joke," and Justin winced, wishing that for once, she'd keep a few thoughts to herself. But then his dad appeared in the doorway, and as always, the man's features transformed, same as his mother's from a moment before. Nearly thirty years of marriage, and the two of them still acted like newlyweds nearly every day.

"There's my girl." His dad's words might have been casual, but his tone wasn't. He leaned down and kissed Justin's mother on the lips.

"Hey, Dad," Justin said after a second, hoping to remind them both that he remained in the room. "How was work today?"

"Work"—his dad winked as he straightened from the chair —"was as good today as ever." He shifted his gaze to Justin's. "You need to come out soon. Before we're too full due to the holiday season for me to show you this year's changes."

His dad managed Hidden Hideaway, a year-round guest ranch that had activities for every season. It's what had brought them to Silver Creek.

"I will," Justin agreed. Now that the high school post season was over, his daily availability to the players would no longer be a requirement. "Tomorrow okay?"

"Tomorrow works for me." Then his dad's focus turned solely to Justin's mother. "We're going to leave now."

"We'll see you tomorrow," his mom added as they headed toward the door. They left the room side by side, his mother laughing softly at whatever words his father had murmured to her, and Justin found himself again moving to the window.

Relationship goals, he thought. If a relationship was what a person was after.

He then peeked back out the window, but he realized that he was no longer the only one peering from house to house. Bree stood at her own kitchen window—which was positioned directly opposite his—and her gaze was now locked onto *him*.

Relationship goals, he thought again.

Then he blinked to reset his thinking. *Friendship goals.* Because he could get behind that. And it suddenly seemed long past the point of getting over actions which had occurred during one minor blip of time . . . and just being friends again.

He couldn't do anything about that tonight, however. The Yarbroughs seemed to be having family night. And anyway, he didn't yet know what he wanted to say. He'd take the rest of the weekend to think about it, and then he'd catch her when she went to meet his mother Monday morning. Hopefully, *before* she ran back out of town.

CHAPTER FOUR

B ree paced the sidewalk outside the new office complex, her fleece-lined knee-high boots leaving footprints in the dusting of freshly fallen snow, and once again mentally flipped through her options for her approach with Mrs. Cory.

Thank you so much for thinking of me. It's truly a great honor to get asked to work with you, and I appreciate it more than you'll ever know. However . . .

You can't know how much it means that you'd ask. However . . .

I'm sorry, but I can't stay in town after all. Because after Saturday night, I refuse to run into your son ever again!

She closed her eyes in continued embarrassment and willed her cheeks not to heat to a bright pink. Justin had seen her practically naked for the second time in his life, and just like three years before, he'd walked away without hesitation.

Stupid man.

Because really, she was a catch!

Not that she wanted to be caught by *him* anymore. But he could've at least done more . . . *said* more . . . than his silent exiting of the building.

She ground her teeth at the memory of her humiliation and pushed the annoying man from her mind. Justin Cory was a non-issue for her. Just like he should have always been. She was way past being over him. Way past caring what he thought.

Only . . . her mind hadn't fully caught up to that declaration. Instead, it had played all kinds of ridiculous what-if games with her since Friday night, especially after learning that he wasn't merely home for a quick visit. He was home to stay.

With a job and everything.

She stopped pacing directly in front of the double doors leading into the lobby and stared through the glass panes. Justin not only had a job in Silver Creek . . . his job was inside this very building.

According to her parents, Justin had finished his physical therapy internship a few weeks before and had taken a full-time job with a local rehabilitation facility here in town. That's why he'd been inside the locker room building the other night. Because the company he worked for had contracted with the high school football team, and during the post season, the coach had wanted someone on-site during all games and practices.

That's how serious Silver Creek took football.

And *that's* why she couldn't consider staying and working on the mural project. Because she wasn't joking about not wanting to run into Justin again. *Ever!* She didn't want to relive her greatest mistake.

And she didn't want to risk her heart joining her mind with the what-ifs.

"You beat me here." Mrs. Cory's easy tone washed over her from behind, and Bree turned to face the approaching woman.

"Mrs. Cory." Bree held out a hand as the other woman stopped in front of her. "It's so good to see you again."

"It most definitely is good." Mrs. Cory squeezed Bree's fingers in hers. "But don't think for a second that you can get away with just taking my hand." She tugged. "Lean down here and give your old art teacher a proper hug."

Bree chuckled as she bent at the waist. "You're anything but old." The familiar scent of her mentor's perfume swirled around her at the same time that two strong arms wrapped her in comfort, and unexpected tears sprang to her eyes. "I've missed you," Bree whispered. She hadn't realized how much.

"And I've missed you." Mrs. Cory released the hug but kept both of Bree's hands in hers. "How have you been, sweetheart?"

A tear slipped down Bree's cheek. "I've been good." She nodded and swiped at her face. Her smile shook. "Really good."

"Yeah?" Mrs. Cory offered her a tissue. "I've kept my eye on you, you know?"

"I know." They hadn't talked in person since Bree had left home, but the woman who'd shown her how to take a love for all things art and shape it into a passion capable of lasting a lifetime had emailed a time or two. "I'm sorry I've not accomplished more already," Bree murmured. Standing there facing her mentor, she worried she'd let her down.

"Accomplished more?" Mrs. Cory nodded toward the door of the building in silent direction, and together they headed that way. "It's not like you've been wasting time, is it? You've traveled . . . studied . . . learned from those who've come before you."

"I have. And I've sold a few pieces, as well."

She pushed the button that would swing both doors wide, and she kept the rest of her thoughts inside her own head. She might have sold a few pieces, but no one had been thoroughly wowed by anything she'd shown them.

"I've seen your work online, too. Impressive selection you've posted."

Mrs. Cory apparently really had been following her. Last year, when yet one more opportunity that had been within reach passed her by, Bree had hired a PR firm to create a website to showcase her work. They'd put some of her more ambitious pieces online, and though a few had sold, again . . . no big wow. Not a lot of return customers.

Her artwork was unique, though. Or that's what she told herself. It fit a niche, and not everyone would like it. Not to mention, given her age, she'd barely gotten started. She had years of work ahead of her. Years to be a success.

Deep down, though, she worried it was neither the uniqueness of her art nor her age that was holding her back. She feared she simply didn't have what it took.

She feared she'd never be anywhere near Beverly Cory.

"We can change things for you," Mrs. Cory said as they passed through the second set of doors and entered the lobby, and Bree looked down at her.

"Change things?" Was the woman reading her mind now?

"We can break you out." Mrs. Cory peered up at her, and Bree quit walking. The woman *had* been reading her mind. "This mural project isn't just about Silver Creek," Mrs. Cory went on. "You get that, right? It's step one of a state-wide historic visual tour. With our 150th anniversary coming up next year, we won the bid to go first, but other cities will be watching to see what we create here. Then they're going to try to up the stakes when it's their turn. That's why you and me, we're going to start at the top, so they have nowhere to go but down."

A small smile tugged at Bree's mouth. She had always loved her mentor's confidence.

"But I need *you* working on this with me," Mrs. Cory added, and the smile left Bree's face. She'd forgotten for a moment that she intended to turn down the offer today.

"I'm still a little undecided, Mrs. Cory." She swallowed as nerves tightened her stomach and dried out her mouth. "I had a couple of other things lined up for the coming weeks."

She had *nothing* lined up for the coming weeks. And also, her parents would be crushed when she informed them that she'd changed her mind about staying.

"Nothing that can't wait, I hope." Mrs. Cory turned her head then, no longer looking at Bree, and Bree followed her line of sight. And she saw where the mural would be created.

In the middle of the modern structure that housed glass walls framed by thick black metal, a three-story wall soared upward. Nothing marred the cream-colored paint on the opposite side of the lobby, and even without seeing the details of the design Mrs. Cory had planned, Bree could already envision it. Silver Creek's history on a wall. The cathedral that sat in the middle of town, miners who'd panned for gold back in the beginning, the surrounding mountains, the creeks and lakes running through the town. Flowers, trees, the local college, the junior hockey team. And so much more. And intertwined in all of it, anywhere that foliage or nature touched, she'd bring it to life.

That's what she and her mentor had talked about. Using the three-dimensional bas-relief sculpting technique she'd once so enjoyed doing—that she *still* did any time she could secure a contract for it—she'd bring the wall to life in a way that would mesmerize everyone simply upon entering the building.

And it would be *her* work being seen every day. *Her* work being admired.

"I see that you can envision the finished product already," Mrs. Cory murmured, and Bree nodded without thinking.

"It could be a showstopper."

Mrs. Cory's hand touched hers, and Bree looked down. "It *will* be a showstopper," she promised. "But only with your name on it."

A rapid heartbeat had Bree's chest rising and falling. She so wanted to do this.

She so wanted to leave her mark in this town she'd always loved.

"I don't know that my actual name would matter," she

demurred, turning back to the wall. "It'll be a Beverly Cory piece. And that'll be enough. That alone will bring tourists into town, will fill up the offices with patients. Just so they can enjoy the beauty while waiting on more unappealing appointments."

"Yes. But you're missing the main point, Bree."

Bree pulled her gaze back to the other woman's. "What do you mean?" What point could she possibly be missing?

Mrs. Cory motioned to the wall in front of them but didn't take her eyes off Bree. "This won't just be a Beverly Cory piece. Your name will be on it, too." She squeezed Bree's hand in hers. "In fact, *your* name will be first."

Her name would be first.

Bree twined her fingers together and gripped her hands tightly in front of her. How was she supposed to turn that down? This project could make or break her.

This project could be all her dreams come true in the matter of six short weeks.

Walking into the building that morning, she'd been convinced that Mrs. Cory asking her to take part in the mural had been done more as an act of charity than anything else. One woman feeling bad that one of her once more-promising students had yet to accomplish anything. But Mrs. Cory wanted to spotlight her.

The ding of the elevator sounded, and the door swished open in front of her. She stepped out of the small space and back into the lobby, then immediately turned to take in the blank wall. She'd just spent forty-five minutes with Mrs. Cory and Mayor Rebecca Garrett in Mrs. Cory's temporary office overlooking the lobby on the third floor, where they'd talked about her contributing to the mural as if it were already a done deal. The three of them had also gone over the proposed design, with Bree immediately seeing ways to amp up several areas to better highlight the bas-relief she'd be contributing. She'd tossed the suggestions out there, unsure how they'd be received, but both of the other women had been enthusiastically on board.

In the end, though, she hadn't agreed to take on the project. Not yet.

But she would. How could she not?

She just needed a minute to come to terms with seeing Justin again first. With potentially seeing him *every day*. And she had to make sure that she was prepared not to once again risk falling for the man her teenage heart would have once done anything for.

"Bree."

Speak of the devil.

She steeled her resolve before turning to face him. "Justin." She didn't know what else to say.

He didn't seem to have any ideas for conversation either, as after he locked his gaze on hers, he then turned and stared at the blank wall on the other side of the room. She didn't follow suit. Instead, *she* watched *him*. And she told herself not to think about how good he looked. Or how much she'd missed him in the last three and a half years.

He sported a trim beard now that was just a touch shorter than his dark hair. His lips were still both a firm slash under a straight nose and as sinfully gentle-looking and kissable as they'd always been. And his lashes remained long, thick, and insanely sexy around his soulful hazel eyes.

Geez, she could so fall under the spell of this man again.

Geez . . . she so had to get a grip, or the next six weeks were going to be both mentally painful as well as sexually frustrating.

She rolled her eyes. She wouldn't let the latter happen no matter what. Because she was over him. It only took one time of offering herself to a man and having him turn her down—while he also pointed out that if sex *did* happen, it would be *nothing* more than sex—for her to get a clue. Justin Cory wasn't for her, and she wasn't for him. End of story.

"Mom tells me you haven't given her a decision yet." Justin finally spoke, and as he did, those soulful, see-too-much eyes turned back to her.

"You've talked to her?" She'd only been gone from Mrs. Cory's office for three minutes.

"She texted as soon as you left. Says I have to make sure you stay in town."

At this, Bree lifted her brows. "*You* have to make sure?" Why on earth would that be the case?

He lifted a shoulder. "She seems to think it's my fault that you never come home for more than a couple of days."

It was.

"*And* my fault that you left in the first place."

Bree stared at him, unwilling to agree to either statement. "And here I always thought of your mother as a smart woman."

At her reply, Justin merely blinked.

"You know that I'd always intended to leave," she pointed out. She also fervently hoped he'd forgotten that she'd also once offered to leave with *him*.

"That's what I told Mom."

"Then I don't understand why you're even standing here."

His jaw tensed, and his eyes went flat like they had Friday night when he'd seen her in the locker room. "I'm standing here because my mother asked me to. Can I tell her your answer is yes?"

He could tell his mother anything he wanted to. But she wasn't telling *him* a thing.

"Come on, Bree." He turned fully to her then, relaxing in his stance, and she could read a hint of pleading in his eyes. "I only have ten minutes before I have to get back to work, so I really need you to talk to me." He motioned toward the wall. "This is a *great* opportunity for you. And I don't want it to be my fault that you don't take it."

Her anger spiked. Why the hell would he assume he had the power to make her miss an opportunity of any sort?

"If you doing this project with Mom means that I have to—"

"My doing it or not doing it," she interrupted, one finger held up in front of him and her not caring a whit what he'd been about to say, "has no bearing on anything I might feel toward you. *Period.*"

"Good." He nodded.

"And for the record, I don't feel a thing toward you." And she wished she never had. "Nor am I displeased that you pushed me away that night. My life has been far better because of it." And clearly, *his* had. Seemed like he'd achieved all his dreams. "So, don't stand there acting like your being in Silver Creek has any impact on me whatsoever. I offered myself to you that night; you said no, and we both moved on. End of story."

His Adam's apple bobbed as he swallowed. "I'm glad to hear that you feel that way." And then he tilted his head toward the wall. "So . . . I can tell Mom you'll be staying?"

His single-mindedness ticked her off even more. This whole conversation really was just about making sure she didn't walk out on this project. It had nothing to do with him wanting to talk to her. Him wondering how she might be after all this time. Or him caring one way or another if she was even there or not. And that alone broke her heart a little. Because she might say that he didn't matter to her, but apparently her heart wasn't listening.

"I'll talk to your mom myself," she informed him. She didn't need him in her business. "You just take care of you . . . and I'll take care of me."

He didn't say anything else, and she expected that to be the end of the conversation. But he also didn't walk away. Instead, he just stood there and looked at her. And Bree found herself holding her breath as she looked back. The two of them had been really good friends once. They'd worked together at Hidden Hideaway every summer since she'd been fifteen. They'd shared secrets, hopes, and fears. And she'd honestly fallen in love with him. So much so that no man since had made as much as a blip on her radar. Not that she hadn't tried—or pretended. But so far . . . nothing.

Thus, the reason she'd intended to sleep with Cord Friday night. Because she needed a blip, damn it!

She needed something more than Justin taking up space in her head.

He shuffled on his feet, and his gaze slid slightly off-center. And then he seemed to be staring at the bank of elevators directly behind her. "I also wanted to say that I'm . . . *sorry* if I interrupted things for you Friday night." He swallowed again. "I could have handled that whole situation better."

Her hold on her anger snapped, and it took everything she had not to growl like an attacking bear and charge the man until she knocked him flat on his back. He wanted to bring *that* up? Did the idiot not know when to just pretend something had never happened?

She leaned slightly to the left, stretching her neck out until he couldn't avoid her eyes any longer, and once she had his attention, she pierced him with a venomous glare. "You mean . . . you *could* have just walked out of the room and minded your own business instead of standing there interjecting yourself where you weren't wanted?"

"*Or* I could have handed you back your clothes and demanded you get off the desk."

A low growl came from the back of her throat, but the dinging of the elevator behind her snapped her back into focus. They were standing in the middle of a public space. With people coming and going all around them.

She didn't need the kind of attention telling him where he

could shove his attitude might bring her. And she didn't want another minute of attention *from* him.

Reining her anger back in, she squared her shoulders and took a small step backward. "It's nice to know where we both stand, Justin. But I *can't* say that it's been nice talking to you. Feel free to let another three years pass before seeking me out again."

CHAPTER FIVE

I t had been over a week since Justin last talked to Bree, but he remained as annoyed now as he'd been at the end of that previous conversation. Annoyed because she so obviously blamed him for how things had gone down three years ago. And annoyed because he still couldn't shake the visual of her sitting half naked on a desk, waiting for Cord Wilde to show up.

But annoyed or not, he *was* happy she'd stayed. And he was also a little happy she was currently in his direct line of sight.

"Should I do the heel slides next?"

"What?" Justin pulled his gaze back from the lobby, which was easily seen from where he stood in the physical therapy office. The patient assigned to him lay on the table in front of him, watching him through big blue eyes.

"The heel slides," the girl repeated. "I forgot about them earlier. Should I do them now or just let them go this time?"

Her question brought a smile to his face. "There will be no 'letting' any exercise go at any time. Yes, do the heel slides." He peered down at her. "And then roll over to your stomach. I want to show you a new exercise to add in for this week."

"Ugh." The girl drew out the word, and Justin patted her on

the forearm.

"It'll all be worth it in the end, I promise."

"It had better be," she mumbled.

Jamie was a fifteen-year-old star athlete on the high school's softball team who'd recently gotten T-boned by another teen driver—one who'd been paying more attention to his cell phone than the rules of the road. In the wreck, her femur had been fractured, but other than a few other cuts and bruises, she'd suffered no additional major damage. She'd been lucky. He knew that firsthand.

"You still think I'll be fully healed in time for spring training?" Jamie asked, and he realized that his gaze had drifted back to the lobby. Bree and his mother had been standing together for the last several minutes, both of them surveying the transfer going on of the image to the wall, and both of them laughing and talking together like lifelong pals.

"I absolutely think you'll be fully healed by spring. But only if you keep putting in the work required to get you there."

The sides of her mouth pulled down. "I will." She dragged the sentence out as if she'd been asked to walk herself to the guillotine. She then flipped over on the small table, and Justin spent the next few minutes testing her strength and flexibility before showing her how to correctly do a prone knee flexion. The girl was already ahead of schedule for where most people with the same injury would be, but he didn't want to push her too hard and cause a setback.

"Is this too painful?" he questioned as she bent at the knee and lifted her foot upward.

She shook her head, her forehead propped on her folded hands and her eyes closed as her face lay two inches from the pad of the table. She was definitely a trooper. And she was obviously intent on doing the work required to get back into top physical shape.

"Let me know if you need to stop. Otherwise, do two slow

sets of ten."

"Got it," she gritted out.

She continued with the exercises, and Justin went back to keeping watch on the lobby. Bree had moved away from his mother and stood at the base of the scaffolding that had been erected late the week before. She looked up at one of the interns his mother had hired to help with the project, and when she smiled at the younger man, Justin's stomach clenched. She hadn't even so much as looked at him in the last week, much less smiled. Not that he necessarily wanted her to. He didn't care if she ever smiled at him again.

Only, he apparently did. Because in the last two days, since Bree and his mother had finally come out of hiding in his mother's office, he'd found himself walking through the lobby at least three times more than his normal routine. And during each pass, though he hadn't so much as attempted to speak to Bree, he'd done his best to make sure she caught sight of him. And each time she did, she turned her head in the opposite direction. The obvious snubs only upped his determination to annoy her even more.

"The decorations are going to be pretty in this building," Jamie said from the table, and he realized that she had not only lifted her head, but she must think his fascination with the lobby lay in the Christmas decorations going up on the front side of the room. It was two days until Thanksgiving, and the town's public lights and decorations in all main buildings would come to life on that day.

"I hear the tree they bought is fifteen feet tall," he shared. He'd overheard his boss talking about it the afternoon before.

"And I hear they plan to dangle mistletoe right in the center of the room."

Justin looked down again and caught a mischievous glint in the teen's pain-tightened features. "You have some interest in mistletoe, do you?"

She waggled her eyes half-heartedly. "I have some interest in Christian Hays. And I happen to know that his daddy works in this building. *And* that Christian comes over here most days after school."

"And if you're going to have to keep coming here three days a week yourself," he added.

"Exactly." She smiled again as she finished her last rep, then dropped her forehead back to her hands.

"That's enough for today," he said as she panted for breath. "I'll finish up with some soft tissue work, then we'll let you sit with an ice pack."

"Sounds perfect," she mumbled into the table, but it took a few more seconds before she had the strength to turn over.

As Justin worked on her thigh, pressing his fingers into the tightened areas while also being careful not to go too far to cause additional pain, he once again turned his sights back to the lobby. And not to the decorations the maintenance people had been busy putting up for the majority of the last week.

He turned his gaze, once again, to Bree, who now sat atop one section of scaffolding, leaning forward so she could better define the outline that had been going up for the last two days. And between snippets of watching Bree, he took in the entire design. It had changed somewhat from his mother's initial plans. He could tell that already, even with only two-thirds of the detail applied to the wall and without any color being added. And it had changed for the better.

Bree was good. He'd talked to his mother a couple of times on his passes through the lobby the last two days, and he'd seen her enthusiasm for what her past student had brought to the table. He'd also spent more than one evening online since the week before, perusing Bree's website. She was *more* than good.

What she had displayed on the website, however, was mostly objects. There was a portfolio of wall art she'd done, similar but on a much smaller scale to what she'd be doing there, but the pieces for sale were different. Still good. Just different. Some were framed artwork that she'd painted, others abstract sculptures—both for hanging or for tabletop display—and there were even regular décor pieces such as lamps and picture frames. But what everything had in common was what she'd be contributing with the mural. Three-dimensional. Nothing she did was flat, and whether she used random objects or plaster and paint, it seemed that was where her biggest talent lay. And that was what he remembered about her skill from before. She saw things with layers of depth that most people never realized, and then she brought those layers out for everyone to enjoy.

The finished mural was likely to be phenomenal.

"Can we do ice now?" Jamie asked from where she lay, and he removed his fingers from her thigh. The girl looked exhausted. He'd put her through the wringer today. However, he wouldn't apologize for pushing her. His promise to himself since he'd started the path to this career was that he'd always do his absolute best to make sure his patients recovered as completely as possible. It was the least he could do.

"Absolutely." He nodded toward one of their therapy assistants, who headed his way. "Shannon will get you hooked up, and then I'll see you next week, okay? Make sure you keep up the hard work over the long weekend."

Jamie nodded without saying anything else, and Justin let the receptionist know that he'd be taking a break. It was mid-afternoon, and the building would be clearing out within the next couple of hours, but given the long nights he knew his mother and Bree had put in the week before, he suspected they'd likely be here for a while longer today. He didn't want to stick around after hours, though. That would be too obvious. So, he'd go out now and attempt to annoy Bree yet again. He had to avenge his annoyance of her avoidance of him somehow.

Dodging a group of people who'd entered the front door of the building and had stopped to admire the artwork going up on the opposite wall, he headed toward his mom. She was currently using a laser pointer to direct one of the interns on the area being transferred from paper to wall, and Justin took a minute to admire not only the work already going into the project, but the effort he knew his mother had put in ten years before to get back to where she could do the job she'd always loved. That wreck had almost taken her out.

He'd thought it *had* taken her out.

So, to be only down two legs instead of six feet under, he knew she was grateful. But he'd forever carry the guilt.

"I figured it was about time you came back out here," his mom said as he stepped to her side.

"You been keeping tabs on me?"

"I think it's more like you've been keeping tabs on *her*." His mom nodded toward the scaffolding, and as if he'd needed to be granted permission, his eyes traveled up two stories to the blonde beauty with her legs hanging off the front of the platform.

Bree wore earbuds in her ears, and with her hair pulled back in a mess of a knot positioned high on her head, he could see the smooth line of her throat. Her top teeth had snagged on her bottom lip as she leaned forward in concentration, with one hand sketching on the wall.

"I'm not keeping tabs on her," he denied, but he knew his mother didn't buy it.

"And I'm not going to point out that you obviously didn't clear the air with her last week."

"I tried." He frowned. "At least she stayed. That's what you wanted."

His mother snorted under her breath. "She stayed because she's not an idiot. But you, Justin Cory, are proving to me that you just might *be* one."

He looked back down at her. "What are you talking about?"

"Like you don't know." She shook her head as if highly disappointed in her only son, then she used her eyes to once again motion upward toward Bree. "She's home, you're home"—she spoke under her breath—"don't you think it's about time you finally tell her how you feel?"

His mother's words couldn't have surprised him more. "What are you talking about?" He didn't *feel* any way.

"Justin, honey. Mothers know these things."

"I don't think you do." Because whatever she thought she knew, she was wrong. Bree had been his friend, and that was all. And yes, he *had* kissed her on her sixteenth birthday. And he'd been wrong to do that. But she'd asked so darned sweetly that he'd been unable to deny her.

That hadn't meant he thought of her as anything other than a friend, though. And he'd never even come close to kissing her again. Well, until she'd shown up half naked in his bed. But seriously, what man wouldn't have considered kissing her at that point?

"I've been married to your father for a long time," his mother said. "And I understand how the heart works."

"Or maybe you're a romantic who can't understand how it sometimes *doesn't* work." And that was the real issue. Ever since the car wreck when he'd been fifteen, his heart had quit working. At least in the romantic sort of way.

Friends? Yes.

Colleagues? Absolutely. He definitely cared about friends, colleagues, and acquaintances. *And* his parents.

But he didn't "feel" things like normal people. Not anymore. And he couldn't imagine he ever would again.

In the next moment, Bree turned from where she'd been working, one hand on the cross bar above her as she started to pull herself to her feet, and when she leaned over as if to say something to his mother—a wide smile on her face—her gaze landed on Justin.

Her smile slipped first . . . and then her foot slid off the edge of the platform.

CHAPTER SIX

"I told you, I'm fine." Bree forced herself not to completely growl the words out because Justin had just dragged her through the doors of the physical therapy office. And everyone inside was suddenly looking at them.

"You're not fine," he insisted. He led her past the receptionist desk. "You sprained your wrist trying to keep from slipping off that blasted thing."

"You're not a real doctor. You don't know what I did." She tugged her good arm, trying to get him to let go of her, but he didn't budge. He just kept walking with unwavering determination through the middle of the floor where at least eight patients and even more staff watched their every move. "Where are you taking me?" she gritted out.

He reached an open door in the back of the room and motioned for her to go inside. "To *privacy*." He spoke under his breath. His eyes bore into hers.

She didn't want privacy.

And she didn't want to be in privacy with Justin!

But her wrist also throbbed like a mother, and she was slightly terrified that she'd done more than sprain it and would therefore lose her one and only chance to make something of herself. And if that were the case, being alone in a room with Justin would be the least of her worries.

She didn't give in yet, though. "Just let me leave," she whispered instead of walking through the door. And darn it if tears didn't threaten to fill her eyes.

"Just step into the room," Justin returned, his voice coming out equally as quiet.

No other sound could be heard throughout the office, and Bree knew when she'd been bested. Either she continued resisting and looked like a fool by refusing to step inside the room that was obviously set up for patient treatment, or she went against her usually spot-on inner mode of self-protection and stepped in the den with her arch nemesis.

She pressed her lips into a tight line. Damn him. She didn't want to be alone with him, and he knew it.

But darn it, she needed someone to look at her throbbing wrist!

"Fine," she bit out. Then she stepped across the threshold and kept her back to the door.

Deafening silence followed after the door softly clicked closed behind her, and the darned tears that had threatened returned. Why did seeing him have to still upset her so much? It had been over three years!

Yet ever since he'd walked into—and then right back out of—that locker room . . . all she could think about was wanting to go back to *before* she'd turned eighteen. Back to when he'd been her best friend. Even though she'd also been in love with him.

She missed him. And she hadn't even known it because she'd been too busy hating him.

"Please let me see your wrist," Justin said, and Bree's heart kicked into a gallop. He was just trying to help, her logical brain told her. He was just being Justin. Not overly nice because it was her.

"I promise you, it's fine." She tucked her "fine" wrist into her chest, and when she glanced down at it, she could see that it was already swelling. When she'd started to slip from the scaffolding, she'd instantly reached out with her free hand—which was connected to the wrist that was now hurt—and had ended up twisting it at an odd angle. She'd kept from falling, though. But getting down hadn't exactly been easy. Especially when she'd insisted that she could do it by herself.

"It's not fine, and I know it," Justin rebutted. His voice took on a tender note. "I saw the way you bent it when you caught yourself. It has to be hurting."

She wouldn't have *had* to catch herself if the man hadn't been stalking her over the last two days. Every time she'd turned around, it seemed, he'd been passing through the lobby. "Why do you have to keep coming out there, anyway? It's your fault I almost fell."

"Wrong. Your stubbornness caused you to almost fall. If you weren't so determined not to even look at me, you wouldn't be in this predicament."

It took everything she had not to turn around and *glare* at him right then. "*Fine.* I'll admit it, then. I don't want to look at you." She stared at the blank wall in front of her. The room had no windows and only an exam table and a single chair as furniture. "Is that really news to you, though? And since I've now said it, does that mean you're going to walk out of here and leave me alone?"

"No."

She sighed. Why did the man have to be so stubborn? At least his annoying behavior had dried up her threatening tears.

"If you don't want to show me your wrist, then I suppose we can just talk," he said, and she closed her eyes in frustration.

"I don't *want* to talk to you, Justin. Don't you get that?"

"Okay. Then I'll talk, and you can listen."

She didn't want to listen either.

47

She didn't want to be there, period!

"Other than you telling me last week to stay away from you for another three years, we haven't spoken since the night you ran out of my room," he began. "We never talked about what happened that night."

"Nothing happened."

"Or what you *wanted* to happen."

She sighed again. Then, with her eyes still closed and with a growing need for him to shut his mouth and keep it that way, she turned and shoved her aching wrist in his direction. "Here." She squeezed her eyes shut tight. "Look at my wrist if you're so hell-bent on it. Just, for the love of God, *stop* talking."

"Then look at me."

Damn him.

Her eyes snapped open, and fire raged deep inside her. "I don't want to look at you, Justin! Why can't you understand that? I don't want to see you and have to remember what a fool I was. I don't want to look at your face and hear you telling me again that I don't matter to you. That what I said that night . . . what I offered—" Her voice broke, cutting off her words, and she shook her head, realizing all that she'd blurted out. She didn't want to be around him because she was incapable of keeping her darned thoughts to herself.

And now she looked like an even bigger fool than she had the night she'd taken off her clothes and thought she could convince him that he loved her, too.

He had yet to look at her wrist, and as he stared back at her, a look of shock marring his sculpted features, her blasted tears returned.

Dang it! Why couldn't he just leave her alone?

"Is that what you thought all this time?" he said. Then he shook his head. "I never said that you don't matter to me, Bree. *Never.* How could you even think that? You've always mattered. Since the first day I met you."

"Except for on *that* night."

"That's not true." He took her injured wrist in his hand, holding it gently but still not looking down at it. And then he covered it with his other hand. "I said no that night because you *did* matter. Don't you get that?"

She let out a dry laugh. "That's a nice line." A tear slipped over her cheek.

"It's not a line, sweetheart." He reached out and swiped the tear away with his thumb. "If you hadn't mattered, I'd have slept with you without hesitation. I'd have *taken* your virginity."

At that statement, she looked away, but Justin reached out and turned her face back to his.

"And then I'd have slept with you *again*, Bree. As many times as you'd have let me. You're crazy sexy, refreshingly real, and probably the best damned thing to ever walk into my life. So, yeah. I'd have slept with you. And then I'd have taken and taken all summer long. *Until* it was time for me to go back to school."

She stared at him, her eyes still brimming with tears, in shock over the words coming out of his mouth. If he felt that way about her, how could he have *not* felt as much for her as she had for him? "But then you'd have just left?" she asked, confused. "Without me?"

He nodded, and she could see sadness in his eyes. They turned a darker shade when he was sad. She'd forgotten that. "I'd have just left, yes. Because I can't offer more. To anyone. And I told you that a long time ago."

"You told me that you had one focus. And that after you finished your education you planned to come back to Silver Creek because of your mom. Because it was your fault she had the accident."

His sadness transformed into nothingness in a split second. He'd pulled a curtain down over his emotions. "But it's not just her who changed that night. Don't you see? It was far from only her who didn't walk away from that wreck the same as she'd gone into it. Far more than even—"

Now it was his turn for his voice to break, and he lowered his head in silence. Bree stood there looking at him, her injured wrist still held by him, and wondered why he thought he couldn't be there for his mother at the same time he could be *with* someone else. What was she missing?

"I don't *feel* things the way other people do." He lifted his gaze and seemed to be begging her to understand. "Not anymore. Ever since that night I just . . . *don't*. I can do friendships, but that's all. That's why I said no that night. That's why I couldn't do that to you. Couldn't take the love you offered while knowing I wouldn't return it. Because I *did* care about you." He put his other hand back over hers. "I *still* care about you."

She didn't know what to say to that. Nor did she know how to feel—or what she thought about his explanation.

But she did know that the massive amount of shame that had been crushing down on her for so long seemed to have lifted a little. It wasn't that he'd flatly turned her down. That he thought her stupid for thinking there was more between them. He'd turned her down to protect her. And that made the whole thing slightly more tolerable.

CHAPTER SEVEN

B ree wrapped her scarf tighter around her neck and pulled it more securely up over her head as the brisk evening air snaked its way inside her jacket, then she veered from the sidewalk running along the front of her parents' house. If she went any farther down the street, the streetlight might catch her, and she'd be visible from the house next door.

She stepped carefully over the trimmed clumps of her mother's prized flowers and tiptoed her way in the dark across the front lawn. When she reached the door, she quietly slipped in, not turning on any lights. She didn't go any farther than the living room, though, before she grabbed a blanket off the couch and hurried back out. The back light burned bright, so she couldn't go through the house and come out the back door, and additionally, she'd have to sneak around the far side of the house, or again, she might be seen from the Corys'.

Where she was headed still sat in complete darkness. Snow was forecast for later that night, so very few stars were out, and it was a new moon. The perfect night for sitting on the swing and contemplating such things as the fact that she'd avoided her parents on Thanksgiving Day simply because she couldn't handle the thought of going next door when they'd been invited.

She'd lied and said that an old friend had invited her over instead.

And then she'd driven around for hours, visiting old haunts she hadn't spent any time in over the last three years.

Rounding the back corner of the house, she headed straight for the swing and was within three feet of it, blanket already wrapped around her shoulders, before she realized that her favorite spot wasn't empty.

She stopped and stared, her shoulders stiffening at the same time.

"Evening, Bree." Justin spoke from the darkness.

"What are you doing here?"

His teeth flashed briefly in the night. "Probably the same thing as you."

At that, she glanced over to the Cory house and could make out their four parents through the windows of the back door. They sat around the kitchen table, the food and dishes cleared, playing some kind of board game.

"They still as gushy as ever?" she muttered.

"Gushy doesn't begin to describe it when you get the four of them together." Justin patted the space he'd left empty beside him and shot her a silent invitation. And though it went against her better judgment, she dropped into it. She had to sit somewhere, she told herself.

Of course, it wasn't just her parents she'd been avoiding tonight. And now she was sitting directly beside the other person on that list. Ever since she'd blown up at him two days before, she'd had trouble holding on to her anger, so now it seemed even more imperative to stay away from him.

But how could she? He was her friend. Or . . . he once had been. And she was pretty sure he could be again. If she wanted to go down that route.

She decided not to worry about that particular aspect of her life at the moment, however, and just appreciate the fact that watching both her parents and Justin's exude love like four mating lovebirds wasn't high on either of their lists. They'd been known to slip out to this very spot many times in the past because one or the other of the couples was making them nauseous.

"So, where did *you* go tonight?" He leaned back and looked up through the trees hanging over the swing. "Aside from the obvious, anywhere but near me."

She neither acknowledged nor denied his comment. "I drove around mostly. The Christmas decorations are pretty this year."

He tilted his head and looked at her. "When's the last time you've been home for Christmas?"

"I come home every year for Christmas."

"Okay, then when's the last time you've been home for the whole *season?*"

He knew the answer to that, so she let it go unanswered. She did slide farther back in the swing, though. And she let some of the tension that had been in her spine since she'd first seen him sitting there relax. It was cold out tonight but sitting in the dark in her favorite spot was just what she needed. Even *with* Justin there.

And possibly because Justin was there.

"Where'd you ditch your car?" he asked when it became clear she didn't intend to say anything else, and she looked over at him in the dark. Her eyes had adjusted enough that she could make out most of the details of his face, and his lips, sexily framed by the scruff of his beard, didn't look nearly as chilled as hers felt.

"At the church at the end of the road," she admitted. "I might have implied to my parents that a friend invited me over. So, I'll have to walk back to get it before they come home."

"I can drive you if you want. It's cold out tonight."

At that she laughed. "We're *sitting* outside in the cold, Justin. I can handle a short walk."

"Fine. Be stubborn." Before she could tell him to look in the mirror, he picked up her right hand. It was still wrapped in an elastic bandage past her wrist, with only her fingers protruding. "How's the wrist?"

"Much better." She flexed her fingers and felt no pain. "I've kept it wrapped and been icing it every few hours. Just like the doctor ordered." Her voice held a hint of teasing, and Justin's lips curled up at the edges.

"I'm not a real doctor. Someone pointed that out to me recently."

"No, but you did seem to know what you were doing when you examined my wrist the other day." Once she'd calmed down enough to actually *let* him examine it, anyway. And when she had, she'd been impressed with the knowledge he seemed to have procured.

He removed the clip holding the bandage together and began slowly unwrapping it.

"So, you've accomplished all your dreams, huh?" Her voice inched up a notch, revealing that her nerves had suddenly gone jittery. And her nerves grew even more so with each additional inch of skin that got exposed. "Became a PT and found a job back here?"

"I've headed down the path I wanted to." The unwound bandage pooled in his lap, and once he'd freed her, he slid both of his hands gently over her wrist. And now her pulse joined her nerves. She also didn't understand how his hands could be so warm. He wasn't even wearing gloves.

"And what comes next?" she croaked out.

"What do you mean?" He looked into her eyes as his fingers probed her still-tender flesh.

"I mean . . . what next?" She nodded toward the garage where he lived and sucked in a much-needed gulp of air after he glanced in the direction she'd motioned. "You have the degrees. The job. You're living back in Silver Creek. What's next?"

"Oh." He turned back. "Next." Then he shrugged. "I don't know."

He returned her hand to her, placing it carefully on her thigh, but he didn't offer to rewrap it.

"I guess I'll just work."

"Sounds boring."

His eyes roamed over hers, the stillness in them making her feel a little sorry for him. He needed to get out and live a little. "It's not traveling around the world, I suppose. But I like my job."

"And that's all you ever want out of life?" She couldn't help but push the subject because after giving it some thought, she'd found his proclamation that he couldn't *feel* like other people did absurd. So he carried guilt about the accident? So what? A lot of people had baggage. Justin had apparently pushed his mother to take him somewhere the night of the accident, even though it had been snowing hard that night, and when she'd met another car on her side of the road in the middle of a curve, she'd lost control. And that sucked for both of them. *Royally.*

But his mother was living a good life. And just because Justin felt guilty, that shouldn't mean he didn't get to live a full life as well. Especially after growing up with parents who did nothing but fawn all over each other. That's the thing that stuck in Bree's head. She couldn't fathom that Justin could ever be satisfied without a love like his parents. She and he may both hide from that much gooeyness on occasion, but she also knew that they both appreciated the love their parents felt for each other. And she couldn't believe Justin's mother wouldn't want that kind of love for him, as well.

"The job is all I ever want," he confirmed. Then he declared that her wrist should be good to go by Monday morning, and he got up and walked away.

❅

Justin stared at the racks of clothes in front of him, all surrounded by women with their arms already loaded down, and asked himself for about the one-hundredth time that day why he'd suggested he join his mother for her annual after-Thanksgiving shopping trip in Helena. He didn't even like shopping.

And he certainly didn't like doing it with a city full of bargain-hunting crazies.

"Do you think your father will like this one?" His mother had moved to his side and held up a plaid button-down.

"I think Dad would like anything you get for him."

She gave him a haughty look. "And I think you're still a little salty over your decision to come with me today."

He stared down at his mother. "Don't say salty, Mom. You're too old to talk like that."

That made her laugh. And *that* made all the bargain hunters look their way. But only briefly. They quickly turned back to the seventy-five percent off racks and got back to business.

"How about 'stay in your lane,' then?" his mom teased, and Justin couldn't stop himself from rolling his eyes. "Sorry not sorry?" she continued. "Throwing shade?"

"Mom. Stop." He pushed her to the next rack before she could move herself. "Why are you trying to talk like people thirty years younger than you, anyway?"

"I'm just trying to stay hip, J."

He rolled his eyes again. "Wrong decade. And you've never called me J. Don't start now."

"It almost made you laugh, though."

At her reply, he realized that he *had* been salty today. And for once, he couldn't blame his mood on Bree. Even though he'd walked away from her last night when she'd been trying to push him to admit that he wanted more out of life than a job and a hefty heaping of guilt, that hadn't put him in his current foul mood. The weather had. And that's why he was out with his mother today, and why he'd have done the same one hundred times over if similar circumstances had presented themselves.

Though he knew his mother was a good driver, he also knew that if he *could* help her on snowy days like today, then that's what he should do. That was one of the reasons he insisted on living in the same town as her, after all. He wanted to be able to be there when she needed him.

But being a good son and having to spend hours shopping during Black Friday?

Well, that would tax even the *best* of sons.

"The struggle is real, eh?"

At his mother's words, he merely closed his eyes. He loved his vivacious mother. And at times, she reminded him so much of Bree. But man, could she drive him crazy when she wanted to.

"You ready to bounce?" she said when she got no response, and he finally cracked.

He smiled down at her upturned face. "What's gotten into you today, Mom?"

"Maybe it's *who* got into me last—"

"*Stop!*" He held up both hands as his voice echoed loud enough to be heard on the other side of the store, and everyone in the entire place looked their way that time. Which only made his mother cackle like a kid.

"Love is a good thing, son." She patted him on the forearm. "When are you going to admit it?"

"I've never said it wasn't." He took the plaid shirt, added it to the rest of the pile he had tossed over his shoulder, then pushed her toward the nearest register. "And whether you're really ready to *bounce* or not, that's exactly what we're doing."

"Fine by me. But I can roll myself, you know?" She said the words, but he noticed that she didn't try to take control.

"And I can roll you faster," he muttered. He just hoped she was done for the day and wouldn't try to get him to stop anywhere else. He'd originally thought he might purchase some Christmas gifts today himself, but it hadn't taken long to remember why he preferred online shopping. He'd go home, wait for the best deals to pop up online—or not, it didn't matter as long as he could do it from the comfort of his couch—then click until his finger got tired.

Bells chimed off in the distance as he closed in on the line at the register, and a Santa could be heard outside the store's entrance to the mall. And though most days he'd have taken the time to stop and appreciate the joy being displayed for the season, his gaze had caught on the snow once again coming down outside. He needed to get his mother back home before it got too dangerous.

"Do you see any other registers open?" He craned his neck to look around as he asked the question.

"This one is fine. We're not in a hurry."

"I'm just ready to go."

They finally made it up to the register, and the second his mother had finished paying and he grabbed her bag for her, he took off rolling her toward the door.

"What's eating you so suddenly?"

He supposed he could at least be glad that she hadn't tossed out more millennial slang. "I just want to get us home before the snow gets too bad."

"We'll get there in plenty of time, Justin. It's just a little snow."

He kept his opinion to himself, and when they stepped outside and he told her to wait on the sidewalk while he went for the van, she promptly ignored him and started down the ramp.

"*Mom*," he pleaded. "Please go back. It's snowing."

"And I have my snow tires on." She didn't pause in her trek across the parking lot until he quickly caught up to her and tried to push her again. At that, she pulled back and reversed, turning herself to face him in the middle of the parking lot.

"What are you doing?" he complained. Couldn't she see how dangerous the roads would soon be?

"I could ask you the same thing."

"I'm trying to get you home." He moved to reach for the handles, and she smacked his hands away.

"You're *treating* me like this is my first day in this chair. And I won't have that." She backed away from him a bit more so she didn't have to tilt her head back so far to see him. "You do know that I've been in this thing for ten years now?"

"Of course I know that. Ten years tomorrow, to be exact."

"And what? The anniversary of the day is supposed to be important or something?" She peered up, her eyes narrowing as she studied him, and he could tell when she got it. Her shoulders sagged, and she wore her poor-Justin face. "Please tell me you don't still think about the wreck every year on that day, son."

"What else am I supposed to think about?"

"I don't know." She threw up her hands. "Think about *anything* but that. Your life? What you're going to do with yourself now that you're out of school?"

At that, he stepped back. "What do you mean what I'm going to do with myself?"

"I mean, now that you've accomplished your goals. What comes next?"

What was the deal with both her and Bree asking the same thing? "I'm going to work, Mom. That's why I *had* the goals in the first place. It's why I got the job."

"And you're apparently going to hover over me too much, as well."

There was nothing like true appreciation. He frowned. "I'm just trying to be *helpful.*"

"You're just *trying* to make sure I don't wreck in the snow again," she tossed back. "You do this anytime you're at home and it snows, you know?"

Of course he knew that. He'd even made trips home on

certain weekends over the past six years just because it was *supposed* to snow.

But he wasn't about to admit that to his mother. "I'm not afraid you're going to wreck again," he explained as patiently as he could. "I'm just trying to help."

"Good. Then hand over the keys." She stuck out her hand. "I'm driving us home."

His first instinct was to flat-out tell her no. She was *not* driving; it was too risky. But it was also her van. And she *was* a grown woman—as well as his mother.

A horn honked behind him, and he realized they were still standing in the middle of the parking lot. Both of them began to move, his mother without his help, and they were soon at the van. Neither of them got in, though. Instead, his mother reached out and took his hand in hers like she had when he was little.

"The wreck wasn't your fault, Justin. We've talked about this before."

They'd talked about it many times before. She'd even insisted he see a therapist when he'd had issues being away from home his first year in college.

Therapy hadn't helped. But then, him not going to more than two sessions potentially had played into that.

"Of course it's my fault." He made himself say the words out loud and look her directly in the eyes as he said them. He'd been pretending for years that he'd moved away from that conclusion, but in his own mind he'd never once wavered. "*I* made you take us out that night. *I* lied to you about her parents, saying they'd given permission to stop and pick her up. *I* pushed. All because *I* wanted to have a first date so badly. And now look at you. Look at *her*!"

She watched him, and he could see her growing concern. Her face went extra still when she was concerned. "And *have* you looked at her lately? Have you reached out to see how she is since we moved here?"

He hadn't seen or heard from his first girlfriend since the morning after he'd almost gotten her killed. Her dad—who'd been out of town the night of the accident—had kicked him out of the hospital while she'd still been in a coma, and he'd made it clear that Justin was never to try to contact her again.

Justin didn't say any of that to his mom. She knew how things had gone down that morning. And she knew him well enough to know that he'd stuck to his word. He'd never tried to contact April again. And because of that, he didn't even know what kind of long-term damage she'd suffered. If she was disfigured, unable to walk, unable to so much as eat on her own. All he knew was that she'd lived. And that was only because his mother passed that piece of information along a short time after the accident.

"She is okay, you know?" she said now.

"And how do you know that?"

"Because I've checked up on her, honey." She squeezed his hand, reminding him that she still held it in hers. "And maybe it's time you did the same. Prove to yourself that you didn't ruin anyone's life." She held up her other hand as soon as he opened his mouth. "And no, that night did *not* ruin my life. I'm quite happy. Yes, I lost the use of my legs. And yes, some days that bites worse than others. But I still have my life, baby. I still have you. I have your dad. And I have my art. My life is good. So don't you think it's about time you quit punishing yourself for something you didn't do?"

He didn't know if that would ever be possible. He did know, however, that if his mother would just once be mad at him for his part in things, then it would make it a heck of a lot easier for him to *remain* mad at himself. Because he didn't *need* forgiveness. Two people he'd cared about had almost died that night. He'd thought they were both dead. And then he'd walked away with barely a scratch.

That was unforgiveable in his book. And not even his mother could change his mind.

CHAPTER EIGHT

B ree touched the tip of her pencil to the paper and worked on the top edge of the mountains a little more, adding additional definition to the shading, then she looked back up at the real thing for comparison. The sounds of laughter and helium being filled into balloons drifted down from farther up the street, but that was more of a pleasure than a distraction. She'd missed this time of year in Silver Creek.

The Main Street Christmas Festival was in full swing, and though she'd started out the morning by perusing some of the craft booths and trying a couple of samples at the candy shop, she'd quickly found herself heading to this section of the crumbling stone wall. It had once been her favorite spot in the whole town, and she wanted to make sure she got this view of the mountains just right. It would be a highlight in the mural, so she had to do it justice.

She went back to her sketchpad and flipped to a fresh page. She had yet to figure out exactly how she wanted to pull the detail out on the wall, so she worked on a couple of ideas for the next few minutes.

As she worked, her mind drifted to other sketches she'd done over the years. As well as to pieces she'd created and had pushed to get into galleries. Several galleries had held interest, but in the end, she'd never sold enough to get a standing spot anywhere. She'd also done a few private murals and a handful of bas-relief projects. And now that she was doing another one, she was reminded of how much she enjoyed that particular type of art. Bas-relief had been something she'd started working with in high school and had become quite good at almost immediately. She'd even talked Justin's father into letting her create a nature corner in one of the public sitting areas at Hidden Hideaway. She smiled to herself, hoping it was still there. She'd have to go out and see it before she left.

The thought of leaving had her putting her pencil down. *Would* she be leaving at the end of this? Where would she go?

Strangely, she hadn't given that too much thought.

Her main focus had been coming home to do the project. And then whether she'd stay or not because of Justin. And then *avoiding* Justin.

But she didn't feel the need to avoid him any longer. It was funny what a few days' time could do to change her perspective. The other night in the swing had been nice. Like old times. At least, until he'd gotten up and walked away because he didn't want to talk about how boring his life was.

A noise sounded behind her, and she caught her breath at the same time she realized that she hoped it was Justin. Looking over her shoulder, though, she discovered a girl of six or seven smiling at her as the girl bent to pick up a large red ball. The child's mother watched from a distance, and Bree merely smiled back at both of them.

When she turned back around, she blew out a breath. What a letdown. And yet, she shouldn't be sitting there hoping to see . . . her *friend*. Her Justin.

She blew out another breath. She was a mess.

Her phone dinged, and when she pulled it out of her back pocket, she saw that it was her oldest sister.

How's the Main Street Festival this year?

She moved her thumbs over the keypad.

Perfect. I've missed times like this.

Does that mean you're thinking about staying home this time?

She lifted her eyebrows at the abrupt question. The conversation had certainly gone to the subject of staying home awfully quick. And she knew why. She sent another message.

Tell Mom to lay off me.

Her mother had made murmurs of her sticking around for good, but so far Bree had only overheard them being said to her father. Her mother hadn't come right out and questioned Bree about it yet.

She says you're talking to Justin again.

At the message, Bree sat up straighter. She hadn't realized her mother had been paying that much attention to her. Had she seen them on the swing the other night?

She also hadn't known her mother was even aware that she *hadn't* been talking to Justin for the last three years. He'd come up in conversations a few times, but Bree had always feigned inability to catch up with him during her short stints back in town.

```
Why are you two talking about me and
Justin?
```

```
I wasn't. She brought it up.
```

```
Tell her to mind her own business about
that, too.
```

She quickly erased the last message before sending it. If she told her mother to mind her own business about anything, that would cause the exact opposite to happen. She typed out another reply.

```
Justin and I have always been friends.
Why wouldn't I talk to him?
```

A reply that time was longer in coming, and that fact made her wonder just what all her mother and her sister had been saying. She'd never told either of them that her early mad crush on Justin had eventually morphed into love. *Nor* had she disclosed that she'd snuck into his bedroom and tried to seduce him that night. That had been too mortifying to tell anyone.

But they had asked more than once why she'd suddenly decided to leave town two months earlier than originally planned. And why she'd done so spur of the moment that morning.

Her phone dinged again.

```
Whatever is or isn't—or has or hasn't—
gone on between you two . . . you know
that I'm always here to talk if you need
to, right?
```

She stared at her phone. What did they know?

And how did they know anything?

A Styrofoam cup of steaming hot chocolate appeared in front of her nose, and she jumped as if she'd been caught trying to sneak into the house after curfew.

Then she realized whose hand held the cup, and she quickly tucked her phone away.

She smiled up at her friend. "You brought me hot chocolate?"

Justin wore a grin in return. "I figured you were cold sitting over here. I know how you used to love to get lost in your own head in this very spot, so my guess is that you've been at it for so long you don't even realize how cold your fingers are."

She wiggled her fingers to test his theory, then she realized that it wasn't just her fingers that were chilled. Her butt had gone numb from sitting on the concrete slab lining the top of the wall.

"They are." She accepted the drink from him and wrapped all ten of her digits around the heat coming from the cup. "Thank you."

"You're welcome." He nodded toward the wall. "Mind if I sit?"

"Help yourself."

Before she could move the sketchpad out of the way from where she'd laid it, Justin had it in his hands. And as he settled down next to her, his legs hanging off the opposite side of the wall from hers, he flipped through the last few pages. "I've missed seeing your work," he murmured as he studied them. "You've improved."

She laughed softly. "I hope so. I've been working hard at it the last few years."

"I could tell."

His wording struck her as odd. "*Could* tell?"

He looked up then. "Oh." He smiled once more, only this time looking more guilty than pleased. "I've checked out your website. A time or two."

The idea made her happy. As had knowing that he'd remembered this had been a favorite spot to sit. "See anything you liked on there?"

"I saw a lot that I liked." He lowered his head again and went back to studying her drawings, and she caught her eyes lingering on the top of his head. He hadn't pulled a cap over his dark hair before coming out today, and her stupid romantic heart wanted to run her fingers through it.

She let herself have that fantasy, accepting that it would never come to fruition, and wrapped up her fantasy with a new understanding that they really were just going to be friends. And she would be okay with that. Her past infatuation would eventually die off completely, and from the other side of it would hopefully emerge a more mature friendship. One that could grow over the years instead of being sidetracked by her teenage imagination.

"I can't wait to see what you do with the mural once you start working on it."

She sipped her hot chocolate and waited for him to look back up. When he did, she gave him a secretive smile. "I take it you haven't stopped by your office building this weekend?"

"No. We're closed until Monday."

"Too bad."

"Why?"

Her lips curved again. She'd enjoyed being in the building the last two days by herself. "Because I've already started working on the wall," she confessed.

"But I thought . . ." He looked at her wrist. "Weren't you going to wait until tomorrow to get back to work? Give your wrist a few more days to heal?"

"No. You only told me to wait. But you're not a real doctor, so what do you know?"

He chuckled at that, and he went back to flipping through her sketchbook. He didn't seem to be paying attention to the pages any longer, though. "And you never did like being told what to do, did you?"

"Exactly."

He closed the book and set it on the wall beside him, and his eyes glittered in the afternoon sun. "Well, I can't wait to see it."

"Then that's truly going to suck for you."

"Why is that?" He laughed again, and Bree found herself thoroughly enjoying their back and forth.

She leaned in as if to share a secret and whispered, "Because there's now a curtain covering the entire wall." Or, at least, there would be before the morning. Mrs. Cory had scheduled that to be done today. "No one will get to see the wall again until the big reveal."

"Is that so?" He leaned in, as well, and his breath mingled with hers. "But I happen to know the artists. And something tells me they might just let me sneak a peek."

She shook her head slowly. "Doubtful."

"You think?" His lips curved even more, and she reminded herself that he was just a friend. That he would only ever be a friend.

"What I think is that you're not so special, Justin Cory."

He laughed at that. Then he put some distance between them. "You're probably right about that. How about a bartering system then? I do something for you . . . you let me see the work in progress afterward."

That had her sitting back, too. "What kind of barter?"

"A party." He looked mildly amused with his answer, as if he knew he already had her hooked.

"What kind of party?" She loved parties.

She loved dressing up, talking to everyone.

Some of her best creative ideas came from being in the middle of a crowd of people.

"The kind where you put on a pretty dress and get to talk until your voice is hoarse."

"*Oh*, the best kind." She put one hand flat on the top of the wall and leaned in once again. "And *where* is this party you speak of?"

"At my father's guest ranch."

She sucked in her breath. She'd just been thinking about going out there.

"The only issue is that you have to go with *me*," Justin added, and she remembered how much he *didn't* like parties. He much preferred staying in during almost any situation. "It's my office party," he explained. "Next Saturday. Since I'm so new, I feel like I have to go. So, I thought you might like to go, as well. Enjoy the dinner and all the pomp and circumstance."

"Of course I would. But"—she eyed him carefully—"isn't that the sort of thing you take a date to?"

"I don't have a date." He looked back at her. "I have a friend."

And having a friend was nice. She nodded without putting any additional thought into it. "Then thank you very much for asking. I'd love to go to your party with you."

"Great. So, it's a . . . *deal*?"

She smiled at his near-miss of saying the word "date" and held out her hand to shake on it. "It's a deal."

CHAPTER NINE

He had no idea why he'd made such a deal. What had he been thinking?

And what was he supposed to do now?

It was Saturday night. Bree had just walked into the garage where his car was parked, and his eyes had just about popped out of his head.

She. Was. Breathtaking.

She was more than breathtaking. She was sex all wrapped up in soft red with a fuzzy white neckline and cuffs. Only, the neckline was around her shoulders—leaving her shoulders completely bare—and the dress clung to every last curve she owned.

And she owned *plenty* of curves.

"Sweet Jesus, Bree."

A grin the size of Montana popped onto her face. "You like?" She did a half curtsy in front of him, before spinning in a slow circle, showing him that her backside was as firm and rounded as her front.

He was a dead man.

"I . . . uh." He licked his lips. "That's . . . *fuck*."

She laughed, the sound as tauntingly sexy as the curve of her red-painted lips, and his dick made a move behind his freshly ironed pants as if it thought it had been handed a personal invitation to come out and play.

Friends, he reminded himself as Bree opened the passenger door and slid inside.

Not friends with benefits.

Unless she wanted to be.

Oh, shit. He couldn't suggest that to her. He'd just recently gotten her to even talk to him again. But good God, how in the hell was he going to be able to think of anything else tonight?

Sending up a prayer that his hormones would take a nosedive off the nearest cliff and into the coldest water, he opened his own door and climbed in. Only, that put him close enough to be wrapped in her smell. And sweet heavenly mother, she smelled as good as she looked. This was going to be the longest night of his life.

"So, tell me about the people you work with," she said as he put the sedan into reverse and backed out of the garage. "Who am I going to meet tonight?"

He kept his eyes focused on driving and refused to let himself think about how her thick, white beaded necklace looked more like some sort of kinky—but classy—sex dungeon dog collar. "Well," he began. Then he had to lick his parched lips again. Was she intentionally trying to turn him on? Was that what was going on? He *had* told her last week that he thought she was crazy sexy and that he'd have taken her to bed every which way to Sunday three years ago if he hadn't cared too much to hurt her.

Maybe she wasn't as okay with how things had turned out as he'd thought since that conversation. And maybe this was her new way of getting back at him. Public punishment with a side of raging blue balls.

"Justin?"

He looked over at her. "What?"

"Who am I going to meet tonight?" Her brown eyes

surrounded by long, thick lashes and smudged with smoky makeup went perfectly with the whole ensemble. It upped her level of sexy to world-ending inferno.

"My boss," he forced out. Then he pulled in a deep breath and made himself concentrate on creating a running stream of polite conversation instead of on what he'd rather be doing.

Twenty minutes later, he turned into the entrance to Hidden Hideaway and made his way to the parking lot of the main building. He pulled up to the valet, and the waiting man had the passenger door open before Justin shifted into park. And this time, Justin had the pleasure of watching someone else look like a gawking teenager.

"Welcome to Hidden Hideaway, ma'am."

"Thank you." Bree smiled sweetly as she let the other man help her from the car, and Justin once again sent up a prayer to get him through the night.

"The party is inside and down the hall on the right," the valet said as he took Justin's keys.

"Thank you."

He moved to Bree and rested his hand at the small of her back as they headed for the front steps, and as he once again breathed in her scent, he reminded himself that he had *not* invited her tonight as a date. He'd invited her because he hated parties, and he knew that she was just the opposite. She'd think the whole event would be fun. And having her there with him would remove the pressure of needing to be overly talkative.

Plus, asking her to the party was the exact type of thing he would have done back before their friendship had jumped the tracks.

"Thank you for bringing me tonight." The red ornaments dangling from gold swirls at her earlobes swung as she turned her head and spoke to him. "I bought this dress last year, and I was worried the only place I'd get to wear it to this season would be my mother's and father's living room on Christmas morning."

The pads of his fingers slid against the fabric as they walked. "You could wear it to the mural reveal. It would certainly garner plenty of attention there."

"Oh, no. I have something better planned for that."

Good Lord. He couldn't imagine what could be better. He reached out and opened the door and stepped back for her to enter. "Would you like to go immediately to the party or look around the place first?" He peered down at her. "I assume you haven't been out here in a while?"

The thrill of looking around was obvious in the way her eyes sparkled. "I haven't been out since I left town." Then she glanced toward the sounds coming from down the hall. "But I do love a good party."

He chuckled. He would have put money on that. "Tell you what, then. Let's go into the ballroom, have a few drinks, do the whole mingling thing, and whenever you get tired of talking, I'll take you around." He shot her a wink. "I happen to know where the keys to every room are, so if something we want to see is locked up, I can still get you inside."

The smile that lit her face couldn't have made him happier. "That'll be the perfect ending to the night."

No, he thought. The perfect ending would be taking his friend to bed.

And *that* was the last thing he needed to do.

Bree hadn't had so much fun since prom night. Justin's colleagues certainly knew how to throw a party. She'd danced with several of them throughout the evening, including a few of the women, and had even coaxed Justin out on the floor a couple of times. She'd also talked to her heart's content. She loved people, and that was one of the reasons she'd always wanted to travel instead of either going to college or just settling down somewhere. There were so many different types of people to run into, everywhere she went.

What she didn't like, though, was *not* having a place that felt like home. But with her and Justin having cleared the air, she now knew that anytime she felt like coming home again, she could do exactly that. And nothing would be awkward about it.

"Thank you again for bringing me tonight." She spoke as the current song ended, grinning up at him at the same time, and noticed how the earlier brightness to Justin's gaze had dimmed slightly. He'd neither done nor said anything to indicate he was ready to go, but she knew him well enough to understand that the poor guy needed a break. Or, at least, he needed to be in a room that didn't have loud music playing in it and wasn't filled to the gills with people trying to talk over it.

"You're welcome." He gave her a small smile. "And thank you for coming. You definitely made the evening tolerable."

That was probably the sweetest thing he could have said. She dipped her head. "I'm glad to be of service to my friend."

"And *I'm* glad we're friends again. I've missed you, Bree."

She'd been wrong. *That* was the sweetest thing he could have said. "I've missed you, too. Come on." She slipped her arm through the crook of his elbow. "Let's get out of here. Take me on that tour you promised."

"Yeah?" A flicker of excitement returned to his features.

"Yeah." She laughed and leaned into him. "If I wasn't with you, you'd have probably left already anyway."

"About two minutes after I first came in," he muttered, and as both of them snickered together, heading toward the main doors, the photographer who'd been hired for the evening stopped them.

"Oh my God, y'all. You're just the cutest couple. And that dress"—the woman took in Bree from shoulders to toes —"honey, if I could do to that number what you do, I'd have fought you for it the minute you walked in here tonight." She held up the camera in her hand. "Can I get a picture before you go?"

Bree looked up at Justin, and he was already nodding in agreement. He also seemed to be looking at her with lust in his eyes again. The way he had when she'd first gone over to his place and he'd gotten a look at her dress.

Maybe the mention of her outfit had reminded him what she looked like in it. And yeah, she looked good. She knew that. But she hadn't worn the dress to try to get Justin's attention. At least, not consciously. That had just been a nice bonus.

"Come over here," the photographer said, motioning them to the corner. "The lighting is better."

They did as asked, smiling and mugging for the camera with the kind of joy the entire evening had been, but before the other woman finished, she pointed upward.

"Now I need you two to kiss."

"What?" Bree and Justin spoke at the same time.

The woman pointed up again. "You're under the mistletoe. Let me get a shot of you kissing."

Bree froze. She didn't want to put Justin on the spot . . . and she also wasn't sure she *wanted* to be kissed. Not even a quick peck. She'd spent the entire evening working hard to remind herself that they were just friends. That they'd only ever be *just friends*.

Did just friends kiss under mistletoe?

"We're not . . ." Justin began, but then his gaze snagged on hers, and they seemed to be asking a question.

We shouldn't, she tried to communicate back. But her eyes turned traitor on her. Instead, what they said was, *Yes. Kiss me, you big lug. I'm going to combust right here in this dress if you don't put your lips on mine now.*

"Okay," he whispered, seemingly to no one, and then his mouth lowered to hers.

Pictures may have been taken; she couldn't say for sure. And the music may have continued to play. But all Bree knew was the feel of Justin's lips on hers, and the touch of his fingers sliding across her cheek and burying themselves into her hair.

She went up on her toes, and he brought his other hand to her face, as well. And he held her there, their lips touching, and she thought back to the first time he'd done this when she'd been sixteen. It had been her first kiss, and she'd had to beg him to do it. It was all she'd wanted for her birthday. But the kiss had been as sweet and tender, and as heart-wrenchingly mind-melting as this one tonight.

He eventually pulled back, staring down at her as if in awe. And for just one second before he blinked and looked away, she thought she'd seen a flicker of something more than friends.

CHAPTER TEN

Two days later, and Bree's heart still raced every time she thought about Justin's kiss. And honestly, she'd thought about it *a lot*. Enough that if she were seeing a cardiologist, they'd probably put her on some sort of medication to help. Because damn, that had been some kiss.

And damn, there hadn't been a follow-up one.

In fact, what they'd done immediately after the kiss was first to take an embarrassed bow when they realized that everyone standing around them had not only turned to watch but was also clapping in admiration. And second, they'd gone on about their tour of the place as if nothing whatsoever had happened in the ballroom.

They'd wandered throughout the main building, checking out the gift shop where she'd once worked, then over to the dining hall, the sitting area where she'd seen the bas-relief she'd created five years before, and then part of the way down to the barn. They hadn't made it all the way because the trail had become too muddy, but she had been able to catch a glimpse of the sleigh used for the horse-drawn sleigh rides. She'd been on the inaugural ride when Mr. Cory had first added them to the offerings at the ranch, and that memory would forever hold a special place in her heart. It had also been the first time she'd looked at Justin and realized he could be so much more than a friend.

Of course, she'd quickly explained her thoughts to him, and he'd wasted no time in pointing out that with her being only fifteen and him nineteen, that wasn't going to happen.

He hadn't said it was a bad idea, though. Just that she'd been too young for him.

She pulled out her phone and brought up the picture she'd snapped of him in his suit Saturday night. He wasn't too old for her now . . . but that still didn't mean anything had changed. Not even the way he made her heart thunder in her chest just from a quick glance.

She blew out a breath and tapped the screen to send him a text. Her heart could beat fast all it wanted, but she'd learned her lesson. She wasn't getting sucked into pinning her hopes on Justin Cory again. They could go on as they were; just being friends. And someday, maybe . . . Well, maybe she'd find someone else who could make her heart go pitter-pat.

She thumbed out a quick message.

```
Come on back. Everyone else has left for
the day.
```

Thirty seconds later, the edge of the curtain that hung around the entire three floors of scaffolding shifted, and Justin's face appeared.

"You're sure?" he asked.

"A deal is a deal."

He hadn't glanced behind her yet, as if afraid to take in what she and his mother had been working so hard on.

"Come on." She held her hand out and headed his way as if he were a little kid and needed help crossing the street. And after she grasped his fingers in hers, she tugged him to the middle of the space and then had to turn him to face the wall before he'd look.

And then he didn't say a word.

As she waited, she found herself holding her breath. Did he not like it?

The base colors were up, and the interns had already knocked out a hefty chunk of the more intricate work in the sections they were taking care of, but as for her portion, there was no color applied yet. About fifty percent of the initial application had been completed, but she still had to come back through and add the majority of the detail. That's what she'd started on today, and what she'd be working hard to finish up that week.

But even only partially completed, she knew this would be her finest work. The trees already looked so real it would make a person want to reach out and touch them, and she could envision kids thinking they could step right onto the stones running along the river's edge.

This type of art, she'd decided earlier today, might just be what she'd been looking for all along. She'd been reminded of that Saturday night when she'd seen the sculpture at Hidden Hideaway. Recognizing the skill she'd already honed back then, she'd been proud, but then to compare it to what this would eventually become . . . it gave her goosebumps. She'd tried so many variations of art over the past years, and possibly what she was born to do had been staring her in the face all this time.

"You're either going to have to say something"—she finally broke the silence—"or be prepared to give me mouth to mouth when I fall over from holding my breath waiting to hear what you think."

He took a small step back and tilted his head up as if to take in more of it. But still, he didn't speak. He did reach out, though, and wrap his hand around hers. And then he held on.

"Bree," he finally whispered. He turned to face her, and the astonishment glowing back at her made her heart feel three sizes too big. "This is *amazing*."

"It's ..." She shrugged. "Not done yet."

"I know. And that's part of what's so amazing."

Her breathing situation didn't get any better. He kept hold of her hand as he turned back to the wall, and when she reached over and rested the fingers of her other hand over the base of his, she could feel his pulse pounding similarly to the way hers did whenever she thought about Saturday night's kiss.

"No wonder my mother was so insistent you be a part of this."

Nothing he could have said would have affected her more. "This is basically your mother's vision."

"No." He shook his head, and then with her hand still in his, pulled her forward and through the legs of the scaffolding until they were on the other side. And then he just stood there and gazed up. "This," he said, "is all you. I see your vibrance and your happiness. The exuberance you have for life. All of that is on this wall. And this isn't even done."

The words brought tears to her eyes.

"My mother is a genius for bringing you in." He looked at her. "*You* are a genius."

When tears slipped over her cheeks, he finally turned her loose, and using both of his thumbs, he wiped her tears away. Then he wrapped his arms around her and pulled her tight against his chest.

"Freaking genius," he mumbled.

More tears trekked down her cheeks, but she didn't bother to catch them. Instead, she wrapped *her* arms around *his* waist. This might be the only time she got to hold him like this, and she wasn't about to waste a moment of it.

They stood like that for several minutes before she sensed a shift in him. She could hear a couple of people pass by in the lobby, likely on their way out of the office for the day, but mostly she heard nothing. Just felt Justin's heart beating.

"Bree." His voice came out scratchy and unsteady.

"What?" she whispered in return.

"I enjoyed kissing you Saturday night."

She swallowed, unsure what she should say. Finally, she nodded, her head still tucked against his chest. "I enjoyed it, too."

"I know I've previously said we shouldn't do that."

She waited, afraid to guess where he might be headed.

"But I sure as hell wouldn't complain if the opportunity arose to do it again."

Do it again? Like . . . now? And to what extent? What would more kissing mean? She didn't want to read too much into it.

Her breathing grew shallow.

"What do you think?" His hand caressed over the top of one ear, brushing a lock of her hair back. "Would me asking to kiss you again totally destroy the friendship we've been working to rebuild?"

Friends didn't kiss. Not like that.

Unless it was a friends-with-benefits thing. Was that what he was asking for?

She knew she had to say something, but her mind kept spinning in circles. Justin had gone still as he waited for her to reply, and her chest squeezed tight as she tried to sort through her thoughts. A friends-with-benefits thing wouldn't exactly be the end of the world. In fact, it *could* be the solution to her worries.

Lose that nagging virginity . . .

Help hers and Justin's friendship grow even stronger . . .

That last one was probably stretching the limits of a good excuse to be kissing her friend, but she left it on the list. Because if they *could* do a casual thing . . . who's to say it *wouldn't* strengthen their friendship?

"Bree?" He sounded worried, and when he finally pulled back, she looked up at him.

But she still couldn't utter a sound. She merely nodded. And his body went rigid. "You're sure? Because we don't have to. You can totally forget I said that."

She covered his mouth with her hand, and then she nodded again. "I'm positive. Kiss me, Justin. Like you did Saturday night."

He stared at her for a moment longer, as if he couldn't believe she'd really agreed to it. And then her vision blurred as Justin's mouth lowered to hers.

He took his time again, same as he had Saturday night. Only this time, their bodies were wrapped together, and she could feel the tension still running through his limbs. He was obviously holding back, but the second his lips had touched hers again, she'd decided she didn't want either of them holding back. She wanted this. She nudged his lips with hers, silently pleading for more, and when he angled his head the tiniest fraction further, she ran the tip of her tongue over the seam of his lips.

He jolted at the touch and briefly pulled back. But he didn't go far. His hands had framed her face again, and his eyes were now a mask of heat and desire.

Then his mouth was back on hers, and nothing gentle remained between them.

He parted her lips, his tongue immediately pushing inside, and they groaned at the same time. As he feasted, she reached up and wrapped her arms around his neck. She needed to feel more of him, along the full length of her body, and as if he understood, he lowered his hands to her hips, and cupping the curve at the base of her butt, he lifted and pulled her in tight. And there was no doubt left in her mind as to whether the kiss was having the same effect on him or not. He was hard and long, pushing against her lower abdomen, and she decided she might die on the spot if this turned out to be *nothing* but a kiss.

"Justin," she begged. She needed so much more from him.

"I don't want to stop," he returned. His mouth left hers to seek out the side of her neck, one hand trailing up her side at the same time, and her entire body lit on fire. This was what she'd been looking for the last three years. And this was what she'd known it would be like with Justin. Their first kiss five years before had hinted at it, but when compared to what they had today, that had been nothing but a snuffed-out match.

"I need . . ." She let her words trail off. She couldn't say it. The last time she'd offered herself to him, she'd been rejected.

He seemed to understand anyway. "I need too, Bree."

He kissed her again, his movements slowing and his mouth making love to hers in a way no other man had, and she reminded herself to hold on tight to her heart. She wanted this. Even if it was just for tonight. And she was determined she could come out the other side unscathed.

"Tell me what you need from me," she whispered the second he paused to pull in a breath. "You can have it, Justin. But you have to tell me."

His eyes had turned a dark green, and he once again held her face in his hands. As he stared down at her, heat and need and desire all rolled into one, she offered a tiny smile that she hoped would convey that this would be okay. He could take whatever he wanted, and she would be okay.

She didn't know if it was true or not, but she hoped so.

"I need *you*, Bree." He traced a thumb over her lips. "I know it's not smart. And I can't begin to promise anything. But I want you in my bed. Under my body. Wrapped around me." He pressed a kiss to her lips and whispered, "I need to make love to you tonight. Worship you until the sun comes up again."

She'd said yes. He still couldn't believe she'd said yes. He couldn't believe he'd suggested it!

Beautiful, vibrant, best friend Bree was going to be in his bed.

He turned into his parents' drive, watching behind him as she turned one driveway behind him, and then he hurried to the garage. He had no clue if what they were about to do was the biggest mistake of his life, but as he'd been standing there, holding her in his arms while looking at the beauty she was transferring from her soul to the mural wall, he'd known it would take a stronger man than him to casually walk away tonight.

She parked and immediately headed his way, and though he caught sight of his mother through the kitchen window, he didn't let that stop him. Now that he'd made the decision, he had to have Bree under him soon, or he was going to lose his mind.

"You haven't changed your mind?" he asked as she entered the garage, and he pushed the button to lower the door.

"Not a bit."

He didn't ask again. He kissed her before they could take another step to move toward his apartment, and it was all he could do not to take her on the concrete floor. But he had a perfectly good bed waiting upstairs, and he was determined they could get to it.

When he pulled away and started up the stairs, her hand in his, she followed. But before he could open the door, she tugged on his arm and stopped him. Late afternoon sun filtered through the window in the stairwell, highlighting particles of dust in the air, and he couldn't miss the concern now tightening Bree's face.

"What is it?" he asked. Had she changed her mind?

He'd stop. He'd do whatever she wanted.

But, oh Lord, how he hoped she hadn't changed her mind.

"I need to tell you something first." She suddenly sounded as young as she'd been the first day he'd met her, and the desire that had been hot in her eyes ten seconds before had dimmed. Replacing it was worry, and that had him turning fully back to her. He interlaced their fingers and nodded encouragingly, never taking his eyes off hers.

"Tell me anything, sweetheart." Whatever she was worried about, he'd take care of it. "What do you need? What can I do?"

"You can make love to me," she told him. "That hasn't changed." Then she pressed her lips together, and pleading filled her eyes. "But before you do, I have to let you know that I'm still a virgin."

CHAPTER ELEVEN

Justin stared back at her, his eyes as wide as her heart pounded fast, and she bit her lip as she waited to see what he would say. And he didn't say anything at first.

Finally, his mouth opened—but then it closed.

Then it opened again. "But you were in the locker room that night. *Naked.*"

Crap. She'd forgotten all about that. She'd been planning to lose her virginity with Cord.

"Yes," she drew the word out. "I *was* in the locker room. *Partially* naked." She knew the "partially" part didn't make any of it any better. "But that was just a moment of weakness. I was coming home to stay for more than a few days for the first time since I'd left, and I . . . I guess I didn't want to come back being the same stupid girl I had been when I'd left."

Not that getting naked and trying to seduce Cord had been any smarter than getting naked and trying to seduce Justin had been.

Geez, she needed a new move. She only had 'get naked and ask nicely' in her repertoire.

"And I guess," she continued, pushing aside the fallacy of her thinking, "if that had happened with him and me . . . well, it would have felt like things were changed somehow."

It would have *felt* like she hadn't still been waiting on Justin to figure out he loved her.

He let go of her hand, and she quickly reached for his.

"No." She shook her head, refusing to let him back away from this. "That doesn't change *anything* that's going on here tonight." She stepped up onto the same step with him and molded their bodies together. "I'm *not* still a virgin because I was saving myself for you this time, Justin. That's not what this is about."

"Then explain it to me." His hand tightened on hers. "Because you've been all over the world, Bree. You're full of life. Gorgeous. Outgoing. How has that not happened yet?"

"It just hasn't." She didn't want to do it with just anyone. Not until she'd known she had to come back home and face her worst embarrassment. And honestly, had she talked Cord into it that night, she suspected she would have regretted it.

Actually, she suspected she wouldn't have been able to talk him into it. Not after he learned what her situation was.

"You want me," she said to Justin. Then she touched her lips to the underside of his jaw and felt his intake of breath. "And I want you," she whispered, nuzzling her mouth up toward his ear. "None of that has changed."

His hands clasped around her waist. "But neither have *I*, Bree."

She closed her eyes and nodded against him. "I know that." She pressed her hand flat on his chest. "This is just sex. You aren't going to fall in love with me. I get it."

He pulled back. "Do you really? Because the last thing I want to do is hurt you."

Lifting her hand, she smoothed it over the line in his forehead. "You won't hurt me." She smiled then, even if it was a little forced. "I won't let you hurt me this time. I won't fall in love with you either."

He studied her a moment longer, but even before he made up his mind, she knew she had him. His pulse raced. And she could feel him once again growing hard against her.

"Make love to me, Justin. Until the sun comes up again."

T hey'd made love until the sun came up—and again just after—and as Bree lay boneless, draped over Justin's body, her cheek tucked against his sweat-slickened chest, she wondered how she'd find the strength to get up and go into work. She was sore in all the right places and exhausted in all the others. And the night couldn't have gone any better.

"By the way . . ." His breath ruffled the top of her hair. "I'm pretty sure my mother is aware this happened."

"Why do you say that?"

"She saw me through the kitchen window when I came home last night. I would imagine she saw you, too."

"Ah." She kept her eyes closed, reveling in both the strangeness and the naturalness of the moment. She'd never woken up with a man before, and she kind of liked it. "I suppose I should tell you then that my mother knows, too. As—I'd assume—does my father."

She felt him lift his head to look at her. "And how do your parents know?"

"I texted Mom before I left the office building last night. I didn't want her to see my car in the driveway and wonder why I never came in." She yawned, covering her mouth with the hand she also had tucked against his chest.

"And you're okay with both of those things?" He dropped his head back to his pillow.

"It's not like we're not adults."

"*No.* But I'm guessing you haven't been in this kind of situation before. And certainly not so blatantly in front of your parents."

She chuckled and slid her arms upward, draping them over his shoulders, and as she did, his palms automatically smoothed up her ribs. "Given how gushy our parents sometimes have a tendency to behave in front of us," she said, "I don't see where any of them could possibly say a word."

The tips of his fingernails skimmed the outer curves of her breasts. "You make an excellent point."

They fell silent again, both in their own thoughts, Bree mostly thinking about how she hoped this wasn't merely a one-night stand. And as she lay there, her gaze fell on the snow now falling silently outside the bedroom window. Justin hadn't closed the blinds when they'd come upstairs the night before. Therefore, the sunrise had been what dragged them from slumber and had them reaching for each other as dawn greeted the day. The falling snow was an added perk of such a blissful morning.

"Is this going to be a one-time thing, Justin?"

The hand that had been stroking up and down her ribcage stalled. "That's up to you, I suppose. I'd love for it to be more. But it also has to be a thing that eventually has an end date."

She licked her lips. "And *why* does it have to have an end date?"

"*Bree . . .*" His fingers at her side curled into his palm, and she pressed her eyes closed.

"I just mean . . . why can't it be open-ended? Why do we have to assume there's an expiration date going into it?" She knew she was treading on uneven ground with her questions, but last night had been too perfect. So she had to ask.

"Well, first of all, I assume you'll be leaving again after you finish the mural. Right?"

She chewed on the corner of her lip. "Probably." She didn't have to, though.

"And what will you do next? Do you have work lined up already? Another country you hope to visit?"

He was making it sound so clinical. Do this, then do that.

Relationships were messy sometimes. And they *didn't* need to be clinical!

She finally shook her head to answer his question, and his hand started slowly stroking over her ribcage again.

"I suspect you'll get plenty of offers after word spreads of the mural," he added.

"I hope so." And she truly did. No matter where those jobs might take her. But why couldn't she know that she had this to come back to when each job ended? "I do want to do more bas-relief. And on a large scale, like this one." Everything she'd been hired to do before the mural had been for single rooms only.

"Then I think that's what you should advertise for. Update your website and feature the mural. Then run ads targeted toward city officials, historic areas, that sort of thing. And once anyone who's in a position to reach out sees one"—he leaned up and kissed the top of her head—"I'm sure they'll come out of the woodwork with contracts in hand."

"Maybe," she muttered.

His hand slid to her butt. "There's no maybe about it. Like I told you last night, you're a genius at this stuff. And the world is soon going to know it."

They fell silent again, but she still wasn't satisfied with the conversation. She knew they'd each have to get up soon to get ready for work, but she needed answers first. Something that explained why this couldn't possibly go anywhere. They were good together. As friends. As lovers. Why end it before they even gave it a shot?

She pulled in a breath, knowing she had to keep pushing. "And what's second of all?"

He lifted his head to look at her again, and she did the same, pushing up with her elbows and propping herself on his chest.

"Second of all," she repeated. "You said that this couldn't be open-ended because 'first of all' my leaving. So, what's second of all?"

"Oh." His eyes clouded over.

"What aren't you telling me, Justin?" That's what it came down to, she was certain. There was something he was holding back. And the only thing she could point to was the accident that had put his mother in a wheelchair.

What else was there about that accident that had changed him so much?

"Will you tell me about the night of the wreck?" she asked, and he stared back in silence. "Give me the details," she encouraged. "That day in your life seems to drive everything about you. Yet, all you've ever told me is that you kept on your mother, begging her to take you somewhere, until she finally caved. Where was she taking you? Or was it something else about the wreck you're holding back? Was it more than that she lost control when she met that other car? Were you two arguing? Did you do something? Did she?"

"Stop." His voice rose, and his eyes flickered with panic. *"No.* Of course she didn't do anything. The other car was in our lane. I saw it. She had to swerve. And the tires simply couldn't find traction."

"Then what am I missing?" She pushed up off him and sat cross-legged on the bed. "Why are you so adamant that you can't love? Or is it just *me* you can't love?"

At her question, his face crumpled, and his hand reached for hers. "No, Bree. It's not just you." He sat up as well, pushing back to the headboard, but not releasing her hand. "It's never been about you. Trust me. If I could love someone, it would *be* you. It would be an honor to love you."

She looked back at him. "Then just love me. I'm right here. All you have to do is let yourself."

He shook his head. "It's not that easy for me."

"Then tell me why."

And finally, he nodded. He told her about his first girlfriend, and about how they'd planned their first date for months, just waiting for her dad to give permission. And when he had, snow hadn't been far behind it.

Her parents got stuck that day returning from an out-of-town funeral and couldn't make it back home, but Justin told his mother they'd given permission anyway. One thing led to another, and his mother's car had ended up rolling down a ravine. He'd awoken in the dark, the snow still falling outside the car, and no other sounds coming from within. And he'd been one hundred percent certain he'd just killed two of the most special people in his life. It had taken until they'd gotten him to the hospital to accept that neither were dead, but what they'd told him had been almost as painful to hear. His mother had been paralyzed from the waist down, and his girlfriend was in a coma.

"Justin," she whispered his name as he finished, unsure what else she could possibly say. Opening her arms, she was gratified when he leaned forward and let her close them around him. This strong, sweet, tough guy that had always been so dear to her thought he'd caused all of that.

She didn't try to tell him any different. Not today. She suspected his mother had already tried many times over. What he needed at the moment was likely simple compassion. So that's what she offered.

"How did your girlfriend turn out?" she asked after several minutes. "What's her name?"

He eased back. "April. And I don't have a clue. She lived, at least." He seemed so broken. "She transferred to a larger hospital soon after, and Mom found out at some point that she'd come out of the coma. But I don't know anything more than that. I don't even know if she's in a wheelchair like my mother . . . or if she's worse."

She squeezed his hand.

"So, that's why I'm unable to love." He said the words so matter-of-factly that if her heart wasn't already breaking, that alone would have done it. "It's not my choice. Since the wreck, I simply haven't come close to feeling that deeply for anyone. I think that part of me just turned off that night. But I'm okay with that. Because I came out lucky with only *that* injury."

CHAPTER TWELVE

Only two more hours remained until the end of the workday, and as had happened every day over the last week, Justin found himself more ready than usual to call it quits. Hopefully, Bree wouldn't be working late again tonight, and he'd take her out to dinner before they settled in at his place. Since she'd awoken in his bed the week before, she'd done the same each morning. Only, for several of those nights, she'd come in late.

Most evenings, though, her lateness hadn't slowed their exploration of each other. She may have never had sex up until a week ago, but she seemed to be anxious to make up for lost time. Not that he was complaining.

"What do you think, will the doc let me go to only two days a week?"

Justin looked up from his laptop where he'd been updating Jamie's report for her scheduled follow-up appointment and gave the girl a smile. "I'm going to recommend it. You're doing great."

"Good." She tugged the oversized pair of sweatpants she'd worn in earlier over her feet, then back over her brace and the exercise shorts she wore for therapy. "Because this place is cramping my style."

He chuckled. This place cramped most people's style. He nodded toward the glass windows that overlooked the lobby. "I thought you liked coming in here so you could 'accidentally' run into Christian Hays."

She glanced over her shoulder at the gaily decorated space. "Yeah." She sighed and turned back. "If only that were the case."

"You've not run into him?"

"Only once. But I see him most days that I'm here."

"Then what's the problem with making sure you bump into him?"

She shrugged. "I don't know. I think he might be avoiding me."

As she spoke, sitting to put her tennis shoes back on, Justin caught sight of the boy in question walking through the lobby. He stopped directly under the oversized mistletoe hanging strategically in the center of the space, then he slowly turned his gaze to Jamie.

Justin didn't point this fact out. Instead, he waited to see what the kid would do next.

"I heard that you kissed that artist under some mistletoe, though," Jamie announced, pulling Justin's gaze back to hers.

"Where did you hear that?"

She rolled her eyes. "In here. Everybody was talking about it last week."

How had he not heard himself being talked about?

"Rachel even showed me a picture."

Justin looked at the receptionist, who had the decency not to try to hide her guilt. "I showed it to several people. It made a heck of a shot."

"I also hear you're dating her now," Jamie added, then she scooped up her backpack and pushed herself to her feet. "*And* that you took her on a sleigh ride out at Hidden Hideaway Friday night." She pursed her lips and peered at him. "Does she like you as much as you like her?"

Who did this kid think she was? "What makes you think I like her more?"

She looked at Rachel, who held up her cell phone with the previously mentioned picture displayed. "A picture is worth a thousand words," Rachel quipped.

He eyed both of them—then took the phone to get a better look at the photo. She was right, his body language read "more" in the picture. In fact, his body language read *more* than he'd ever realized he was capable of.

But then, they were talking about Bree. How was he supposed to *not* be crazy about her?

"Why don't you two worry about your own love lives?" he grumbled and handed the phone back.

Rachel shrugged. "I don't have one."

"And I'm too young to have one. I'm simply trying to get kissed under the mistletoe."

She noticed Christian in the lobby then, and her spine went straight.

"He's out there," she whispered from the side of her mouth.

"And he's looking at you," Justin whispered back.

And he was *still* looking at her. Then, as if the clouds had parted on an overcast day, a shy smile flashed across the boy's face before he ducked his head, and Justin thought Jamie might faint at his feet.

"You'd better get out there, Cinderella. I think your prince might be waiting."

She tossed him another roll of her eyes, in obvious disgust with how totally uncool he was, but quickly headed for the lobby. The only problem was that young Christian decided to move, as well. He didn't go far, but he no longer remained under the highly anticipated mistletoe, and when Jamie "bumped" into him, he actually lingered long enough to have a conversation.

Justin watched a minute longer, hoping she didn't give up on the kid too quickly. Sometimes the shy ones needed a bit of extra help. He brought his attention back to the report he'd been working on, then noticed that Rachel still watched him.

"What?" he asked.

"You like her."

He looked back up. "How could a person not like Jamie? She's a terrific kid."

She shook her head. "I'm not talking about Jamie." She waggled her phone in the air, along with waggling her eyebrows, and he narrowed his eyes.

Glancing toward the lobby, he wished he could get a glimpse of Bree. Then he held out his hand and asked to see the photo again. And damn, it *was* a heck of a shot. He was leaned in toward Bree just a hair, both of his hands gently cupping her cheeks, while her fingertips brushed against the front of his chest. He hadn't even known she'd touched him, he'd been so fixated on her lips.

And he'd give a mint fortune right at that moment to have her touch him again.

"Where are the pictures the photographer took?" He cleared his throat, trying to be subtle about the fact that his voice had come out croaking like a frog and peered over the phone at Rachel.

"I got a link to them earlier today. I'll download them as soon as it slows down in here."

He nodded. "Let me know when you do." He wanted to see what the other shots looked like.

His phone buzzed with a message.

Can you take a quick break?

Looking toward the lobby, he asked Rachel when his next appointment was.

"Not for another ten minutes."

He didn't see Bree anywhere. Sure, he typed out. I've got ten minutes. Where are you?

Can you meet me in your mom's office?

Closing the laptop, he asked Rachel to text him when his appointment came in, then he took off toward the stairs. That would be quicker than waiting on the elevator.

Coming out on the third floor, he hurried down the hall and noticed that the blinds on the office his mother had been using were closed, and the lights behind them appeared to be muted. He stopped outside the door, looking up and down the passageway, wondering if she'd switched to another office and hadn't mentioned it.

He didn't see any other signs of either Bree or his mother, so he rapped lightly with his knuckles and cracked open the door. "Bree? Mom?"

A lamp burned in the front corner of the room . . . and then he saw what he'd been called up for.

Bree sat on top of his mother's desk, nothing covering her body but panties, a bra, and a shirt opened down the middle. Looking exactly as she had that night in the locker room. His dick came to life.

"You'd better not be expecting anyone other than me to be showing up here."

Her smile was pure evil. "Not intentionally."

He growled under his breath. He'd been the unintentional one before, and he hadn't liked it one bit. "*Only* me," he said, and her smile inched higher.

"Only you," she repeated. She nudged her chin toward the door. "If you want to make sure it remains only you, come inside the room and close the door. After all, we only have ten minutes."

So he went inside and closed the door. He also locked it behind him.

And then he didn't stop moving until he had his hands gripped under each of Bree's knees and his mouth fused to hers. It had been nearly twelve hours since he'd been inside her, and that was far too long to have to go.

"You know that your mother has a key to the room, don't you?"

Unfortunately, he did.

Equally unfortunate, that knowledge wasn't about to stop him.

"Then you'd better hope she doesn't use it before I get finished with you."

He pushed the shirt from her shoulders, recapturing her mouth and turning her quick smile into a moan, then he undid the hook at the front of her bra.

Her breasts spilled into his hands, and his thumbs and forefingers immediately tweaked both nipples. She had very sensitive breasts, and he'd found that fondling them could get her to do most anything he asked.

"Unzip my pants," he begged. He didn't want to stop touching her body.

She both unzipped and unfastened, and in the next second, he filled her hands. She stroked the length of him, cupping his balls with her other hand, and the move squeezed her breasts together and arched them closer to his chest. He kept kissing her as he dragged his palms down her back, and when he reached her panties, she did a little side to side shimmy so he could jerk them down without either of them having to stop what they were doing. And then they were both free, and he had to find a damned condom.

"Protection," he mumbled. He reached for his wallet, but she produced one between two fingers before he could get to his own. Then she had the packet open and was rolling the latex down over the head of his dick, and he had to grit his teeth to keep from coming in her hands. "Hurry," he pleaded, and he couldn't help the slight pump of his hips. Which only caused her to delay her actions.

As her hands slowed, he opened his eyes and pulled back to watch her. If she wanted to play this game, he was okay with that, too. He liked it long and drawn out as much as he enjoyed fast.

He gripped her by the knees again, tugging her slightly forward and spreading her legs wider with an obvious push to the insides of her thighs. Then he took one thumb and pressed it in a lazy circling motion over her clit.

"Oh," she breathed out the word and seemed to forget that her hands remained positioned at the top of his shaft.

He slid one finger down her, pushing inside and immediately curling upward, but then just as quickly retreated.

She moaned again. And that time she also gave a little shudder.

"Roll the condom down over me, Bree." He whispered the words in her ear, pushing and retreating with his finger yet again, then adding a second, and felt himself throb as her hands once again began to move.

She still took her time, but he didn't complain. He took the moment to dip his mouth to a breast, lifting it at the same time, and after he thoroughly tongued her nipple, he gently closed his teeth down over the tip.

He nipped, she panted.

And then she finally had the condom in place.

"Ready?" he asked. He knew she physically was. He had the proof all over his fingers. But he liked to make sure she was as hot and needy as him.

She nodded, her eyes closed and her head lolling back, and after he nipped at her nipple yet again and positioned himself in just the right place, he slowly pressed forward.

They both sucked in a breath as he slid inside, and her eyes flew open. Her gaze locked on his, staying there as he continued to slowly push, and when he filled her to the hilt, her lips compressed into a tight line.

"Good?" he asked.

She nodded.

Then he rocked in and out, this time being the one to take his time, and she braced her hands on the desk behind her. He once again gripped her knees and made sure that with each thrust her body fit as snugly to his as was humanly possible, and as he watched a warm flush seep over her body, he silently conceded that he was going to miss the hell out of this woman when it was time for her to go.

"Justin," she whispered. Her eyes drifted closed again, and he kept up a slow thrust.

"Touch yourself for me." He wanted to make sure she enjoyed this as much as he, but he wasn't ready to give up his position just yet. Every push forward jostled her pretty breasts, and every wet-slickened retreat pulled a soft breath from her lungs. He could do this forever.

"Hurry," she mouthed, but the word was soundless. Her fingers tangled in her curls.

"Keep touching yourself." He upped his pace. "And open your eyes when you're about to come. I want you looking at me as we finish together."

She nodded, and her fingers kept working while he continued to inch up the pace. As sweat rolled down the middle of his back, and he wasn't sure he could hold on for two seconds longer, her eyes finally snapped opened.

Hot determination filled her gaze as her body began to tense, and he kept pumping. And then she was exploding around him, her walls gripping and sucking at him from within, and with one final thrust, he sailed right over the edge with her.

It took a moment for them to come back to the present, and

when they did, Bree's evil smile returned. "That was even better than I thought it would be."

"That got even hotter when I heard someone stop on the other side of the door."

Her eyes went wide. "What?"

He laughed with pure delight, unable to hold in the ruse, and as she began to laugh with him, she swatted him on the arm.

"You're evil," she said.

He pressed a kiss to her lips. "Then I'm a good match for you."

They started rearranging their clothes, Justin aware that a message flashed on his phone, but he ignored it. His patient could wait. He didn't know how many more moments like this he'd get, so he wanted to take his time. When she pulled her red bra around her, he pushed her hands out of the way and secured the hook himself.

"Do you know what this bra reminds me of?"

Big brown eyes stared up at him. "What does it remind you of?"

"The bra you wore that night when I found you in my bedroom."

She shook her head. "I didn't have on a bra when you came in."

"Oh, I remember that well. No bra, no shirt—" He ran a finger down her stomach to the top of her panties. "Only a pair of red panties, quite similar to these."

She flushed, and he wondered if she'd picked out her underwear purposefully today.

"But you apparently had *on* a bra when you came into my room that night."

When his meaning sunk in, her eyes went round again. "And I forgot to grab it when I ran out."

He nodded. "You forgot to grab it when you ran out."

"You found it?"

"No. My mother did."

His words sunk in, and the look of mortification that passed over her face made him smile. She was so pretty, whether happy, sad . . . or horrified. "What did you tell her?" she asked.

"Mostly the truth."

"The truth?" She was now mortification times two.

"I had to tell her something, and I wasn't about to tell her I'd started cross-dressing. Plus, she . . ." He shrugged. He didn't want to tell her that his mother had known he'd had the hots for his best friend for years. Even if he *had* known that having them was all wrong. "Anyway," he continued. "That's why she assumed your leaving town right after had something to do with me."

Again, understanding dawned. Her hands dropped to her sides. "I didn't even think about that. That first day when I ran into you here, I was too mad to realize that she shouldn't have any reason to assume my leaving had anything to do with you."

"But as you've said before, you always thought of my mother as a smart woman." She'd said that when they'd been talking about this very subject.

"I wonder if she mentioned it to *my* mom," she mused as she went back to slipping into her clothes. She hopped to the floor, shimmying into her jeans, and he considered the question.

"I suppose it's possible. She didn't ever say anything about it to you?"

"No. But she recently made some comment to my sister about me talking to you again. I hadn't realized she'd known I *wasn't* talking to you."

He gave her a wink. "Seems your mother might be a smart woman, too."

She finished dressing, and he helped her to straighten the desk back to the way she'd found it, and he couldn't keep from wanting to tell her one more secret.

He snagged her hand in his. "I kept it, you know?"

"You kept what?"

"Your bra." When she went silent, he made a face. "Kind of a pervie thing to do, huh?"

"A little." She scrunched up her nose. "Do you have a stash of bras you've collected from different women over the years?"

At that he laughed. "Absolutely not. Just yours."

Her face changed then, going from half concerned to fawning. "Justin." She said his name in a syrupy-sweet voice and reached out and wrapped her arms around his waist. "Then I think that's sweet."

"Not sweet." He wrapped his arms around her, as well. "It's pervie. You're just a romantic."

She turned her face up to his. "I think you might be a romantic, too."

"I don't think so." But if anyone could make him want to be one, it was her.

He kissed her as his cell vibrated with another message. "I have to go. Come with me downstairs?"

"Of course."

As they stepped onto the elevator—because this time he *wanted* to drag out the time it took to get back to the office—she asked if he'd celebrate with her the following night.

"Sure. What are we celebrating?"

The elevator dinged, and the doors opened. "Me finishing the mural."

Instead of stepping out, he turned to her, a kind of excitement he wasn't used to feeling jolting through him. "You're finished?"

"Not yet, but I will be tomorrow."

The doors closed, keeping them inside, but the car didn't move. "That's a whole week early."

"I know." She grinned as if her best prized cow had just won the blue ribbon at the county fair. "But I really enjoyed doing it. I've been so anxious to see the final version done, so that's why I kept pushing to work extra hours. And anyway, the protective coat still has to go on, so it still won't be completely finished. A couple of the interns will handle that."

He pushed the button to open the doors again, and this time when they slid apart, he and Bree stepped out. Then they just stood there, looking across the space at the curtain-covered wall, and pride for what he could only envision filled him. She was so talented. She deserved all the recognition she got from this.

"You going to let me have another peek at it?"

At his question, her eyebrows shot up. "Absolutely not. You're going to wait just like everybody else and be wowed at the unveiling, as you're meant to be."

"Fine." He gave her another quick kiss, then pulled her with him toward his office. "Then will you let me drive you home today?" He'd been trying to get her to ride in with him every day.

"No."

"Come on, Bree." He motioned toward the windows. "It's been snowing for a week."

"And I can drive in the snow as well this afternoon as I could this morning. I am from around here, you know. I've been doing it for years."

He couldn't win anything with her. And he really hated the idea of either her or his mother driving in the snow so much. Yet both of them were insistent.

He had one more idea he thought he could win. Taking both her hands in his, they stopped just outside his door, and he could see Rachel watching them with interest. "Can I cook your celebratory dinner for you instead of taking you out?"

"You cook?"

"I do. But we'll go out if you'd prefer."

Her eyes shone, and he could tell the idea pleased her. "I'd love for you to cook. I've never had a man cook for me before."

He kissed the back of her hand and offered a bow. "Then prepare to be wowed."

CHAPTER THIRTEEN

S he was definitely prepared to be wowed. She just hoped Justin would be, too.

Bree opened the garage walk-through door and stepped into the inner space. Justin had left the door unlocked for her and had told her to come on up when she arrived, so other than to take a moment to stomp the snow from her boots and dust it from her jacket, she didn't slow in heading toward his place. As predicted, she'd finished work on the mural earlier that afternoon. And the high she remained on now was almost magical. She'd come home, spent a couple of hours with her parents since she'd barely seen either of them over the last week, then when they'd left for their own date night, she'd taken a long bath and prepared for the evening.

She wore one of her favorite dresses, along with black knee-high boots with crisscross detailing running up the back, and she was prepared to wow Justin herself.

Quietly climbing the stairs, she rubbed her hands together in anticipation. Tonight wasn't just a man cooking dinner for her for the first time. Nor was it merely a celebration of the completion of the biggest project she'd ever taken on. Tonight, was the start of big changes in her life.

She knocked on his door, not wanting to walk in uninvited even though she'd done so several times over the last week and a half. Tonight was a special date, and she wanted it to be treated as such.

The door opened in front of her, and she immediately saw that Justin had understood the importance of the evening. He'd change from his work khakis and pullover with the office logo to a pair of black slacks and a white button-down. It looked like he'd even trimmed his beard, as well.

"Don't you look yummy," he greeted her. He stepped back, brushing his lips over her cheek as she entered.

"And doesn't this place smell absolutely divine?" The mingling aromas in the room already had her salivating.

"Thank you. I hope you're in the mood for steak."

She shrugged out of her faux, fur-trimmed puffer jacket and let him take it from her. "I'm always in the mood for steak. But red meat isn't what I smell." She sniffed the air and moved toward the kitchen. She'd had no idea he could make a room smell so good.

"No." He followed her. "That's the caramelized pears and red onions you smell. I was waiting on you to arrive before tossing the steaks into the skillet."

At his words, she looked over her shoulder. "Caramelized pears and red onions?"

"Yes, ma'am." His eyes roamed down over her body.

"When you cook dinner for a woman, I guess you do it right, huh?"

His gaze returned to her face, and he gave her a soft smile. "I'm trying. It is a celebratory dinner, after all." Lifting a finger, he circled it in a twirling motion. "Would you mind spinning so I can take in both sides of that dress?"

She smiled in return. "It would be my pleasure."

Lifting her arms to her sides, she slowly turned in a circle, and the appreciation she felt as his gaze traveled over her body-hugging black-and-white sheath dress had her almost suggesting they skip dinner and get right to the dessert. Sex with him was phenomenal, but no matter how many times they did it, she always wanted more.

"You good now, or do you need another turn?" she teased, and he bit down on his lower lip.

"I think I might have implied it before, but I'm going to go on and say it outright tonight. You're evil, Bree Yarbrough. And that dress has diverted so much blood from my brain, I'm not sure I can currently remember how to even cook a steak."

"Then my evil plan worked." Her dress was white down the front, with a black back and a black elongated swirl up one side and over her shoulders, while the other side showcased a geometric pattern curved over her hip that appeared to cinch in at the waist. It was classy and elegant, but with a cutout just above her breasts and another between her shoulder blades, it was also sexy.

He gulped. "Your plan was to skip dinner and let me have my way with you on the kitchen counter?"

She laughed, pure joy rushing through her at the fact the two of them were together. Since coming home with him the week before, her life finally felt like things were starting to gel in just the right ways. "My plan," she corrected, "was to keep you so off-kilter that you don't know up from down."

"Ah." He nodded. "Perfectly executed."

She turned back to the kitchen, the smile remaining on her face, intending to find the pears and onions and take a peek. But Justin's fingers snaked around her wrist, and he turned her back to him.

"Kiss me." He moved in and aligned her body with his. "You can't waltz in here looking like that and not at least satisfy me temporarily."

She touched the tip of her tongue to her upper lip. "And a kiss is going to satisfy you?" She suddenly wasn't just *thinking* it would be hot to skip dinner and go right to dessert. She wanted to.

"Kissing you always satisfies me." He cupped the back of her head and proceeded to demonstrate. And surprisingly, after pulling all the air from her lungs and leaving her legs the consistency of wet noodles, he lifted his head and stepped away. "See?" he said. "Satisfied." However, his voice was no more steady than her legs.

She could go along with his plans for now, though. Because she had things to tell him.

Lifting the lid to the simmering pears and onions, she inhaled, caught a naughty grin from Justin, then turned and after tugging her dress partway up her legs, placed her hands on the countertop behind her and lifted herself up. She settled in on the cool stone, and Justin seemed to forget that he was supposed to be taking care of dinner. She pointed to the meat resting on a plate beside her.

"The steak," she said. Then she rubbed her belly and "accidentally" hiked her dress up a few more inches. "I'm *so* hungry."

His mouth went to hers. "You're *so* evil."

He kissed her again, leaving her as breathless as before, then pulling back with obvious reluctance, he reached for the steak. He seemed to be as air deprived as she, along with the obvious lack of blood reaching his brain.

"I have news," she offered as he turned on the burner under a cast iron skillet, and when his kiss-drugged gaze turned back to hers, she tilted her head and waited for some of his fog to clear.

"What kind of news?" His gaze dipped to the front cutout of her dress.

"The career-building kind."

The words had a focusing effect as he suddenly paid complete attention. "Career building?" He left the skillet to heat and came back to her. "How so?"

She'd only gotten the call that afternoon, and she'd already talked to her parents about it. "I took your advice," she told him. "I haven't had my website updated yet because we didn't want to publicly preview the mural before it's revealed, but I did get a glowing recommendation from your mother and went ahead and reached out to my agent to see what she could do."

"I didn't know you had an agent."

She lifted a shoulder. "It's a new thing." She'd acquired her agent earlier that year after participating in an exhibit in France. "Anyway, she agreed with your points about targeting historic areas and city officials, and though all they have to go on at this point is your mother's recommendation and my current bas-relief portfolio, I already have two major cities interested in hiring me."

"Bree!" He wrapped her in his arms. "That's fantastic."

"Yeah." She kept her hands on his chest as he turned her loose, not ready for him to step away just yet. "They're going to come see it the day after Christmas."

His eyes went wide with surprise, then he wrapped her in his arms again. That time, he didn't immediately pull back. He kissed her instead. And he kissed her in the way a woman with potential career-changing news deserved.

His hand crept under her dress as his mouth fused to hers, and when his fingertips brushed over the place where her panties would normally be, his body went still.

"Bree?"

"Yes?"

"I think you forgot to put something on when you dressed for tonight."

She shook her head and inched forward on the counter. The move required her legs to slide farther apart in order to accommodate him standing in front of her. "I didn't forget. I've just been waiting for you to notice."

He groaned, reached over and turned the stove burner off under the empty skillet, then pulled her off the counter and headed toward his bedroom. With her legs wrapped around his waist, she could feel the length of him already pressing upward, and after he yanked the zipper down the back of her dress, she pulled it over her head.

He dumped her onto his mattress, standing tall and his stance screaming sexual prowess, and she went instantly wet. Unhooking her bra, she tossed it across the room. "You can add that one to your collection."

"I'd love to." He crawled onto the bed with her. "If I take all your bras away from you, I guess you'll just have to go braless all the time." One hand closed around her rounded flesh, and the area between her legs throbbed. "I could get used to these always being unfettered."

"And I could get used to always having your hands on them."

Truth be told, she was already used to it. And she wanted to make sure that never stopped.

She didn't voice her thoughts as he stripped and located a condom, though. Instead, she kicked off her boots, then she welcomed him with open arms. They didn't take a lot of time for foreplay, as if they were both in the same heated rush, and as he filled her body in one hard thrust, her heart overflowed for her friend. She'd fallen in love with him again.

Or, more likely, she'd never *quit* loving him.

Either way, she wanted this to last. She *needed* it to. And as before, she also had no doubts that Justin could grow to feel the same for her. He might not be there yet, but only because a mental block remained due to his past. She saw beyond his pain and fear, though, and she knew that with patience, she could help him overcome it.

"Kiss me, Justin."

He dragged his lips from the top curve of her breast back up to her mouth, and as his lips closed over hers, she dug her fingers into his hair and held him tight. She loved this man.

She would always love this man.

And what better way to celebrate the knowledge than by putting it out there during the potential best day of her life? Everything she'd ever wanted could come to fruition in a little more than a week, and she couldn't wait for it to happen.

Pushing at his shoulders, she rolled him to his back without separating their bodies, then she straddled his hips and took the lead. They'd made love like this a couple of times, and she really enjoyed it. But what she enjoyed most was the power that rising up over him seemed to provide. He was a lost man when she rode him, and it was the most alluring sight she'd ever seen.

She almost told him she loved him right then, but she managed to keep it inside. She needed to give him more time. But she planned to show him how she felt in every way she could.

Stretching forward, she gripped the headboard and let her breasts dangle above his face. And he didn't waste any time in regaining the lead. Capturing a nipple between his lips, his hands went to her hips, and then all she could do was hang on for the ride.

He thrust upward like a man possessed, and she ground down to meet his every move. And when her body suddenly raced toward completion, she worked her hips, trying to keep him in the game.

She came first, but only by seconds, and when she dropped back to his chest, happy tears burned at the backs of her eyes.

Justin's breathing ran ragged for several more minutes, and though neither of them spoke, his hands roamed over her body as his heart rate settled. He touched her like a man who loved a woman, and as usual, she found she couldn't keep everything she felt inside.

"I'm going to stay longer than Christmas, Justin." Her agent had already informed her that any contract she agreed to would take a minimum six weeks to be signed.

"You are?" One hand paused at the curve of her hip. "Why?"

She didn't say anything for a minute. She couldn't.

Why?

Was the man an idiot?

She pushed off him and moved to sit on the bed. "Because of *this*," she answered.

At his blank look, she motioned back and forth between them.

"*Us*," she tried again. "I have nowhere I need to be anytime soon, so I'm going to stay. See where this goes."

She could already see him closing down, and she wanted to kick herself for even bringing that up. But damn it, the man had to get past his issues. She'd tried to get him to talk about them more than once over the past week, but each time he shut her down.

He was broken.

It wasn't his fault.

And she could understand the fear that gripped him at the thought of caring for someone again. Waking up in the dark at the age of fifteen and thinking he'd played a part in killing two people had to have been excruciating. But that shouldn't mean *his* life should have stopped that night.

"Don't you think we've got something worth giving a chance?" she said, and he rose up from the bed and reached for his pants.

"What I think is that we both know the reality of the situation."

"The reality of the situation?" She grabbed her dress off the floor but held it on her lap instead of putting it on. "You mean, that you can't love?"

"Exactly."

"And what if I told you that I think it's just fear driving you?

That you've built walls to protect yourself and you simply have to put in the work to take them down?"

He looked over at her. "Then I'd tell you that you don't know anything about it."

"Oh, Justin." She stood and pulled the dress over her head, reaching back to zip it up. "How could I not? I know *you*. Probably better than anyone."

He shook his head. "You don't know about this. If you did, you'd never imply what you're implying."

She stared at him, floored by the meaning in his last statement. Was the man seriously too scared to even say "relationship" out loud?

Or was it "love" that had him so fearful?

"What about the jobs you're hoping to be offered after the mural reveal?" He tossed the question out as if catching her in a lie as he searched around for his shirt.

"What about them? I can go wherever any job takes me, then I can come home. To *you*."

"But that's not what we agreed to."

She stared at him again, her patience running thin. "Would you *please* quit being so hardheaded for just one minute?" She gritted the question out.

"I'm not being hardheaded. I'm being a realist."

"You're being a *jerk*."

With anger now pushing out her attempt at being understanding, she grabbed her boots and sat on the edge of the bed to pull them on. She knew she shouldn't have said anything about this tonight. He needed to be eased into it more slowly. But at the same time, *why* should she have to treat him with such kid gloves? The man was a grown-up. He should be able to acknowledge that she wasn't just some friend with benefits that he could toss aside without a moment's hesitation.

"Are you going somewhere?" He eyed her boots before sliding his gaze up to hers.

"I'm certainly thinking about it."

"But we haven't had dinner."

She snorted. She didn't give two shits about dinner. "What if I told you that I love you, Justin? What would you say to that?" She hadn't meant to blurt those words out, but there they were. And now she'd just see what he thought about them.

He didn't seem to think anything at first, and she didn't move a muscle as she waited. He took his time slipping his arms into the sleeves of the shirt he'd just picked up, then buttoned each button. And only when he finished did he once again look at her.

"Well?" she prodded.

"I'd say that you're a fool."

A kick to the chest would have been more tolerable. "A fool?" Her desire for remaining in this discussion took a nosedive. He thought her a fool. How dare he?

"Yes. Because that's the thing you told me wouldn't happen."

She stared at him, unwilling to shed tears of either hurt or anger, and slowly stood from the bed. "Okay then. I guess I'm done here."

He offered a shrug and turned to head for the living room. "If that's what you want. I'll talk to you tomorrow."

She stared at his retreating back and couldn't believe she'd fallen for this man again. She couldn't believe she'd thought that *he* might fall for her. Or that she even wanted him to. And clearly, he hadn't. He *wouldn't*.

Pain pushed at her from all sides. She needed to get out of there before she broke down.

And she needed to end things tonight before she got any more inklings that she might someday matter. "You're wrong," she told him as she went for her coat. "You *won't* talk to me tomorrow." If she had her way, he'd never talk to her again.

"What are you talking about?"

"We're finished, Justin. As of this moment. There's no need to keep up the charade of a relationship any longer. And no need to keep seeing each other until I leave town."

As a matter of fact . . .

She whirled back. "Better yet. There's no need for me to stick around Silver Creek until Christmas at all."

"You have to. The reveal is next week."

"I didn't sign a contract to be there. My job is done." And her need to get away from Justin was great. Decision made, she pulled on her jacket. She had a new career to focus on, and Justin Cory wouldn't weigh her down.

"When are you leaving?"

"This apartment or this town?"

His tone went flat. "This town."

"Right now."

They stared at each other, and she could see his issue forming in his head. She didn't let it deter her, though. His issues were not her issues.

"You're not leaving tonight." He pointed to the darkened window. "It's snowing like crazy out there. The roads will be slicker since it's dark."

"So? The slick roads and the fact that I'll be on them is no concern of yours."

"Bree," he warned. *"No."*

No?

She returned to where he remained in the living room and got in his face. "You don't get to tell me no, Justin. You don't get to tell me anything at all."

"I won't have another person's accident on my head."

She shrugged. "Then maybe you should have thought about that before calling me a fool."

She knew her words were cruel. If she for some reason did get into an accident, it would be through no fault of his. But logic didn't rule her words at the moment, and she wanted him to hurt. Just as she did.

"And if I were to wrap myself around a tree," she went on, "or heaven forbid, roll my car down a ravine, that's not on you either."

He flinched as if he'd taken a direct hit, but as she headed for the door, he followed.

"Do not drive out of here tonight, Bree." He was only a step behind her. "You may not make it back."

She waved a hand as if swatting away a fly. "I told you, my leaving isn't on you."

"Really?" He slapped a hand to the door as she reached for it, slamming it back the second it opened, then glared down at her. "It's not on me, huh? So, if I were to say that I love you, too, you'd still go?"

She stopped breathing. What was he doing?

"*Do* you love me?" she asked carefully.

She didn't think he intended to answer, and her subconscious screamed for her to get out of there before he did. But instead of forcing his hand off the door, she turned to face him. And she hoped.

"Do you, Justin?"

The air felt electric as she waited, and finally, he shook his head. "No. I don't."

She stared in utter shock. Unable to fathom that he could be so cruel as to tease her with the words then just knock her feet out from under her. With a small nod, she knew that it was time to walk out of his life. Forever.

"Thank you for telling me the truth." She then jabbed her elbow into the bend of his arm, pulling a grunt from him as the move forced his hand from the door, and she stepped out of his apartment without looking back.

She managed to hold onto her tears until she grabbed a bag of clothes from her parents' house and got into her car, but as soon as she backed out of the driveway, she let the tears flow.

CHAPTER FOURTEEN

"I don't care how many times you ask me. I'm not going to text her because I'm not getting in the middle of this." Justin's mother went on, "You've asked her mother already, and you've texted Bree. That's all you can do. She's a grown woman, honey. She'll let someone know where she is when she's good and ready."

"But what if she's lying dead on the side of the road somewhere?" He paced across the living room again.

"Chances are she's not." His mother's calming words didn't soothe him.

"Well, I don't want to take that chance."

"And I don't see that you have any choice."

She shot a pointed look at the couch, and for the third time since he'd come over that morning, he sat back down.

"What did you do, Justin? Why did she leave?"

Of course she'd take Bree's side. He scowled. "What makes you think I was the one who did something?"

"Because she's more level-headed than you."

He gaped. That statement was unfair. Bree was known to blurt out anything just because the thought had passed through her mind once, as well as take off at the drop of a hat. Whereas, he thought everything through. He contemplated things. He was the level-headed one. She let her emotions rule, not logic.

"Plus," his mother went on, "you ran her out of town three years before, so it makes sense that it might be your fault again."

"She was going to leave *anyway*! We've been over this a hundred times."

"But she didn't have to leave that day." She maintained her annoyingly serene demeanor. "And she didn't have to *not* come back for three years." She looked down her nose at him. "I assume she left here hurt again?"

"I didn't do anything to hurt her."

Her chin jerked slightly, as if his rebuttal had gotten under her skin, but that was the only physical proof. "If I remember correctly, that was your excuse last time, too."

"It wasn't an excuse," he gritted out. "I told you. She tried to seduce me that night. She thought she loved me, and she'd *saved* herself for me." He hadn't shared that information before, and from the lift of his mother's brows, he knew she understood why he'd never fully explained. "So you see," he went on, "it would have been wrong of me to sleep with her back then. Inexcusable when I knew it couldn't go anywhere."

"True. So then, I take it you were prepared to let it go somewhere this time?"

He went stoic. He didn't know why he'd come over to talk to his mother anyway, but he was tired of it. He made to rise, ready to go home. He had to get ready for work. But his mother reached out and took hold of his wrist.

"Sit back down, Justin." It wasn't a request.

He sat, but he refused to look at her.

"Now tell me what happened last night. I saw her before she headed home from work. She was so excited. So thrilled to have completed the mural and ready to celebrate that with you. And I know how great you two are together."

"We've always been friends. That makes it easy to be good together."

"You've also always had a crush on her," she pointed out. "Only, I think it might be more than that now."

She was wrong, but he didn't tell her so. Because he didn't want to have to explain to his mother just how broken he was.

"Did that have something to do with last night? Did one of you want to push things too fast perhaps?"

He turned his head toward the opening leading into the kitchen where he could hear sounds of his father preparing breakfast. He didn't want to admit to his mother that he'd never had—and never would have—what she had with his dad. He didn't want to see her pity for him.

"Justin." She demanded his attention, and he hung his head, unable to fight her inquisition any longer. Plus, wasn't this actually *why* he'd come over? He and his mother had always been close, and when he got right down to it, he needed her advice with this. Bree had left hurt last night, and that's the last thing he'd wanted to do to her. But he hadn't seen any other way to get her to face reality. He'd explained things before they'd ever started sleeping together.

"She told me she loved me," he finally admitted. Then he dropped his gaze to the carpet at his feet.

"Okay." His mother, and her ever-present calm reasoning, could be both annoying and appreciated. At the moment, he appreciated it. "And what happened after that?"

"I called her a fool." The sounds from the kitchen abruptly stopped.

"You called Bree . . . a *fool*," she repeated. "For loving you?"

It sounded so much worse when she said it. "Yes."

"Why, Justin? Why would you do that?"

He could hear not only the confusion, but the protectiveness she'd always felt for Bree simmering inside her words.

He could explain himself, though. Sort of. But even he knew he shouldn't have said that.

He kept his eyes downcast. "Before we started this, I let her know that I wouldn't fall in love with her. That I *couldn't*," he stressed. "And she promised she wouldn't fall for me again, either. That she wouldn't let me hurt her again. But she lied, Mom." He glanced at his mother, but what he saw instead was the look on Bree's face when he'd called her a fool. The word had ripped her apart. "And it barely took a week for her to do it," he went on. "We were just supposed to be having a good time until Christmas. We agreed. And then she'd leave like normal. She would have gone on with her life and found someone who could love her back instead of sitting around here waiting for it to be me." And she *should* do exactly that. He hoped she eventually would.

His dad showed up in the doorway, dishtowel in hand and wearing a concerned expression.

"Why would you think you couldn't love her back?" he asked, and the question surprised Justin. He and his dad rarely had deep conversations. That had always been his and his mother's thing. The question couldn't be ignored, however.

"It has to do with the wreck," his mother answered before Justin could, as if she completely understood.

But whether she understood or not, shame filled him. Both his parents now looked at him as if they felt the same.

"You don't understand," he pleaded with them. "You've always had each other. You've never had to lie in the dark, not knowing where the car had landed, but absolutely certain that the two other people in the car with you were dead. And that it was *your* fault."

"But we *weren't* dead," his mother pointed out.

"And your thinking is a little selfish, wouldn't you say?" Heat now laced his dad's tone.

"I'm not trying to be selfish." Justin started to rise, thinking that might make it easier to make his point. But the way his dad looked at him kept him seated. "It's just how I feel," he went on. He didn't know how to make them understand, but he tried anyway. "Something changed with me that night. I'm no longer able to open my heart like you two can." He'd once thought he'd have a relationship just like his parents. And at fifteen and facing his first love, he'd envisioned that relationship happening with April.

"And you say that's because you woke up in the car thinking your mother and girlfriend were dead?"

"*Yes.*" He wasn't proud of his failures, but he wasn't in denial either.

"And how do you think I felt when I heard that my family had gone down a ravine?" His dad's voice was a harsh slash into the room, his jaw tight. "I thought I'd die inside when the cop showed up at my door. I split open like a damned fish that had been gutted. And I had to wait—*also alone*—to hear word about *both* of you. When I should have been the one driving the two of you to begin with."

"Here we go," his mother muttered, but Justin didn't look at her.

His dad went on. "You think I don't carry guilt because I didn't step up as the man of the house and take you and April myself? My wife was paralyzed that night, Justin. And they had to cut *you* out of the vehicle."

His mouth went dry. He'd never seen his dad in so much pain. And he didn't like it. "But I was barely even hurt, Dad. I was okay."

"And I was sitting at the hospital, wondering how long it would be before someone showed up to tell me to head on to the morgue instead of waiting around for two ambulances."

Justin didn't know what to say. He stood, but he didn't go to his dad. He'd thought about how scary that night must have been for him before, of course. A long time ago. But the man had never said anything like this. He never acted as if the worry from the accident had impacted him in any sort of long-reaching way.

"Why do you think I cherish every day I get with your mother? With you?" He shook his head, the heat from a moment earlier gone. "Don't wallow in the past, Justin. Don't refuse to live because you were scared that one night. I know it was terrible for you. And if I could take the pain and fear that you felt from you, I would. But please, son, don't be afraid to open your heart for fear of being scared again. The worst thing you can do is live simply to be afraid. It's a waste of the opportunity you were given when you *only* had to be cut out of the car that night."

His mother touched his hand, and he looked down at her. "And this is why I cherish your father." She offered an understanding smile. "Whether you think you can open your heart and love or not, I suspect Bree's already worked her way inside there. Think carefully about that, son. Don't let go of someone so special if she's who's meant to be in your life."

"**A**re you sure you won't change your mind?"

Bree ignored the pleading in her sister's voice. "Positive. I'm going to stay here and be your helper." She lifted two bell-shaped cookies from the pastry mat and placed them on the cookie sheet. "You still have several other things to fix today, and I'm an excellent helper."

"Bree." Erica slid a pan of cookies out of the oven and set it on the counter to cool. "It's your big day. You deserve this. You *need* to go home."

She didn't *want* to go home.

Well, she kind of did. But at the moment, she wanted to *not* go more than she wanted to be at the reveal.

"You've worked hard for this," Erica reminded her.

"I have. But I didn't do it for the party at the end. I did it for the love of art. Plus, I have meetings scheduled for two days from now. That's when the big payoff could happen."

Erica finally quit arguing and pulled out the ingredients to make a batch of homemade yeast rolls for the Wilde's Christmas Eve dinner. And Bree went back to not thinking about Justin.

She'd shown up at her sister's door after midnight the week before, and thankfully Erica had been home. With Gabe's house right across the street, that wasn't always the case. But her sister had welcomed her with open arms, as well as a box of tissues, and Bree had poured out her heart. She'd been there ever since, pretending a little more every day that her heart wasn't still flayed wide open and that her anger didn't still register at a 10.0.

Her phone rang, and when she saw that it was her mother calling via video call, she propped the phone up by leaning it against a coffee mug and pushed to connect the call. She kept cutting out the next batch of cookies.

"Hi, Mom."

"How are you, Bree?"

"I'm good." She held up a cookie. "Just helping out for Erica's big day." With this being the first Christmas Erica would spend with her fiancé's family, she'd offered to do a lot of cooking, but she seemed to be happy taking that on.

Her mother's gaze shifted to look over Bree's shoulder as Erica stepped in behind Bree and gave a quick wave.

"Hello, Erica. Are you taking good care of your sister?"

"You know it. Keeping her busy baking. That can stop anyone from having the blues."

"Oh. Well, maybe I need to do some baking myself then. Because I just can't believe that our Bree isn't going to be home for the big reveal today."

"Believe it," Bree inserted. "I *will* be home tomorrow, though." She didn't want to miss Christmas with her parents.

Her parents had been upset when she'd texted before leaving town last week, but their disappointment had been split between

Bree's leaving and learning that Bree and Justin had a fight. They'd been totally on board with that relationship since day one.

"Will you take pictures at the reveal for me today?" Bree asked.

Her mother gave a dramatic sigh. "I suppose I'll have to if there's no way I can talk you into coming home."

Erica spoke up from the other side of the kitchen where she currently had her hands buried in a bowl of flour. "If I can't manage to kick her out of here in time to make it back, I'll drag her to the Wildes' with me this evening. At least that way she won't be alone for Christmas Eve."

"I suppose that's better than her being alone." Her mother had a tone of resignation. "And I suppose there's nothing else I can say since she's already decided to let Justin run her out of town again."

Bree put down the cookie she'd just cut out and leaned into the phone. "What are you talking about?"

"Honey." Her mother's sympathy voice was on point today. "I know what happened on your eighteenth birthday. Mrs. Cory told me a long time ago."

Mortification drenched Bree. She'd *known* Mrs. Cory must have told. "And why did you never tell me that you knew?" Her voice went up an octave.

"You never brought it up, so I assumed you didn't want to talk about it."

She *hadn't* wanted to talk about it.

"*Should* I have brought it up?" her mother probed.

"*No.*" It's just that it was humiliating to know that what she'd thought she'd kept as her biggest personal secret had been known by both hers and Justin's mother. She shot Erica a look. "Please tell me you didn't know about that before now, as well? You didn't let me pour my heart out to you while you pretended to play dumb, did you?"

Erica held up both hands. "I had no clue until last week. I swear."

"I didn't even tell your dad," their mother assured them. "I'm good at keeping secrets when I need to be."

"Good. Then make sure to remain strong if Justin asks where I am again." He'd apparently knocked on her parents' door first thing the morning after she'd left to see if they knew if she was okay. He'd sent several texts to Bree, all saying the same thing, as well.

She hadn't replied to any of them, but she had eventually told her mother to pass on that she hadn't wrecked. Other than that, he didn't need to know anything.

She realized that her mother had gone silent in response to her plea, and Bree groaned. "Tell me you didn't already tell him where I am, Mom."

"I *didn't* tell him. I just . . . well, he's worried about you, Bree. I think he misses you."

"He needs to miss me. He's an ass, and he lost a good thing."

"*Bree.* Quit cussing like that."

Erica made a snorting sound from the other side of the room. They both knew their mother thought Bree cussed too much.

"I know that you love him, honey. So I understand being upset."

She *was* upset. And that hadn't eased one iota over the last week. She just kept thinking about their argument and how he'd so coldly declared that he didn't love her.

She was also heartbroken.

Tears suddenly filled her eyes. "I just want to know why he can't love me back."

"I know, sweetie," her mom soothed. "But love isn't always easy."

"You and Dad make it seem easy."

Her mother scowled. "Me and your father have been at it for a long time." She leaned closer to the phone and lowered her voice. "Trust me, it hasn't always been easy."

"Well, if it's hard for you two, then I'm done with love forever."

Erica had moved to stand behind her again and rolled her eyes at Bree's proclamation.

Her mother shook her head. "Don't say things you don't mean, honey."

But she wanted to mean it.

She wanted to know that she'd never hurt like this again.

"Fine. Then I won't ever love *him* again. Is that better?"

The corners of her mother's mouth pulled down even further. "I don't know. I'm just not ready to give up on you and him yet."

The last thing she wanted to hear was her mother saying that she thought Bree should give Justin another chance. But that's the exact type of thing she would say. Only, how did you give a man a chance who didn't want one?

A knock sounded at the door, and Bree looked back at Erica. Erica held up her still flour-covered hands, and Bree returned to the phone.

"I've got to go, Mom. Somebody is knocking on the door, and E can't go answer it." She disconnected. "You expecting someone this morning?"

"I think Harper said something about running by to sample the cookies early." Harper was married to one of the Wilde twins. And her coming by for a sample made sense because Bree had already had one, and Erica's cookies were to die for.

She went to the door and swung it open . . . but it wasn't Harper standing there. It was Cord.

Bree's cheeks flamed at the sight of him, and upon him realizing it was her, his eyes quickly scanned down her body. When his gaze returned, he offered a sexy smile. "Too bad. You're wearing clothes today."

"What?" Erica yelled from the kitchen.

"Nothing," Bree returned. "He's just joking." Then she shot Cord a silent, keep-your-mouth-shut look. She hadn't shared that particular detail of the night of the football game with her sister.

Cord merely smiled again . . . and then he winked.

Too bad Justin had interrupted them last month. This man was hot.

But then, it wasn't really too bad. Erica had been right all along. Cord wasn't for her. Plus, she was glad it had been Justin she'd had sex with for the first time. Even if he was an ass.

"What are you doing here, cutie?" Cord asked as she held the door wide for him to come in.

"I could ask you the same thing."

"And I could ask if you're seriously in there flirting with Cord," Erica tossed out from the other room.

"He's very flirtable," Bree tossed back.

"Leave her alone, Cord. This one is nursing a broken heart."

The smile fell from Bree's face, and tears once again threatened. Dang it. Why had her sister had to go and say that?

Cord's brows rose at the sight of Bree's now-wet eyes, and Bree shrugged. "The guy who was in the locker room that night," she mumbled.

"I'm sorry." He tilted his head as he studied her. "Did you like him a lot?"

"No. He was just a temporary fixation."

"The bigger problem at the moment," Erica spoke up again, now joining them in the living room while she wiped her hands on a dish towel, "is that she did this amazing mural in our hometown which she'll likely get multiple job offers from—as well as quite possibly becoming well known in the field of bas-relief sculpting—and she says she's not going home for the big reveal today. Because she doesn't want to see Justin."

Cord looked at her with surprise. "You're letting problems with a man keep you from being there to accept the recognition you deserve?"

"It's not like that." She wasn't *letting* Justin keep her away. She'd made that decision for herself. She didn't *need* to be there.

"Then what's it like?" Erica argued.

Bree looked from her sister to Cord, feeling as if she were being ganged up on. But at the same time, a light suddenly dawned. They were right. What had she been thinking? She loved events. And her parents were looking forward to this because the mural had her name on it. Why should she let them down just because Justin didn't want her?

She shot them a wide smile and started backing toward the stairs. "I'll tell you what it's like when I talk to you tomorrow . . . because I'm not letting some man keep me down today."

Erica squealed. "You're going to attend?"

A decision had been made—and Bree's wallowing somehow instantly gone. She quickly checked the time. "Assuming the roads aren't bad, I should have plenty of time to get there and get changed before it starts."

Excitement poured through her. Screw Justin Cory. This wasn't his party, and it wasn't his town. Today, it was hers.

"I need to pack." She headed for the stairs. The place—a renovated fire hall—had only one bedroom, which was on the upper floor, and even though she'd been sleeping on the couch, she kept her clothes upstairs. "I'll call Mom on the way and see if she can steam my dress," she called down as she hurried up. Then she heard someone else knock on the door, and as she dragged her suitcase from the closet, she caught a familiar voice coming from the first floor.

"What the hell are you doing here?"

Justin?

She rushed to the window overlooking the street and looked down. It *was* him. But what was he doing there?

And how had he known where to find her?

"I was just visiting with your girlfriend."

CHAPTER FIFTEEN

J ustin stared at the man standing in front of him. Cord was taller, as well as carrying an extra twenty pounds or so of muscle. But that wouldn't stop Justin from punching him in the face if need be. Such as, if he'd laid so much as a hand on Bree.

"Visiting my girlfriend?"

"You know," Cord said. "The cute blonde who looks *really* amazing in pink panties and a matching bra?"

Justin's temper spiked.

Erica appeared at the corner of the connected kitchen, concern marking her face, and watched the two of them without saying a word. Bree didn't seem to be anywhere.

He turned back to Cord. "I know who my girlfriend is. And I also know a hell of a lot more about what she looks like both in *and* out of clothes than you do." At least he hoped he still did.

"And I know that she said you were temporary."

Hearing that hurt, but he probably deserved it. And it still didn't keep him from wanting to punch the guy in the face.

His hands clenched at his sides.

"Bree?" her sister yelled, and ten seconds later, Bree slid down a fireman's pole positioned between the living room and kitchen.

"What?" she asked. She looked at her sister instead of at him.

"You have company."

She didn't immediately face him, but he couldn't miss the tension that tightened her shoulders. No one said anything else as they all watched her, and finally, she slowly turned. It took another three seconds before her gaze found his.

"Oh . . . it's you."

Dismissal at its best.

Justin looked from Bree to Erica to Cord, wondering what he'd walked in on and just what had been going on here over the last week. "Am I interrupting some sort of party?" he asked.

"Yes," Bree replied simply. "So why don't you go ahead and leave. You weren't invited."

"Or maybe we'll leave." Erica spoke before Justin could figure out how to reply. He found himself grateful for her suggestion, but from the look of rage on Bree's face, he feared she'd kick him out two steps behind them. "I'll take my supplies with me," Erica continued, "and finish up the rolls across the street. Cord? Would you like to join me?"

"Do I have to?"

"I need help carrying a couple of things."

The other man didn't take his eyes off Bree as Erica weighted his arms down with items from the kitchen, and when she was done, Cord went to Bree. He stood directly in front of her, blocking Justin's view. "We'll just be across the street if you need us."

"Thank you," Bree whispered.

Nothing else was said as the two of them left, and once the door closed behind them, Justin folded his arms over his chest. He didn't want to think he was too late.

He also didn't want to think about what might have gone on between Bree and Cord over the last week.

But he couldn't help but think of all of it.

Bree moved to the kitchen, grabbed a dish cloth, and began wiping down the counter, and Justin made himself count to five before saying anything. When he did speak, though, what he said didn't come out any better than it would have five seconds before.

"What the ever-loving *fuck* has gone on between you two this week?"

Bree's dark eyes slid over to him. "Whatever do you mean?"

His teeth snapped together. "I *mean*...why is Cord Wilde currently 'across the street'?"

She shrugged. "I would imagine because his brother lives there."

"Then why was he over *here*?"

She turned to face him, leaning back against the counter, and mimicked him by crossing her own arms over her chest. "Be careful, Justin. All these questions imply jealousy, and jealousy implies that you might care."

"I'm not jealous." What a stupid thing to say. He was one hundred percent jealous.

"Is that right?" She angled her head and watched him. "Then what would you call it?"

"I just don't want him touching you."

"How about if I touch him?" Her casual delivery had his teeth grinding together even more, making him worry that he might crack a tooth.

"I don't want *that*, either."

"Well, it's a good thing this isn't jealousy I'm seeing. Because given your current state of agitation, I'd worry about your blood pressure if you ever had to experience such full jealousy."

He lowered his arms then, knowing they weren't going to get anywhere like this, and he also knew that it was up to him to change things. He'd caused this mess, and he could see that she didn't plan to make it easy for him to try to fix it. He crossed the room, and when he reached her side, he worked very hard not to sound like he wanted to rip someone's throat out. "Did you touch him already, Bree?" He hated asking questions he wasn't sure he wanted the answers to. "Did he touch you?"

Was he too late after all? And if he was, could there be any way to still get her back?

He'd once thought he'd wanted her to walk away from him and find someone who could love her the way she deserved. To not wait around on him. How wrong he'd been.

He could love her the way she deserved.

He *wanted* to love her that way.

"Why are you here, Justin? Why drive all the way from Silver Creek just to tell me again that you don't care?"

He noted that she hadn't answered his questions, but he couldn't let that get in the way.

He pulled in a breath. "That isn't why I came."

"Then why did you?"

This was harder than he'd realized it would be, but only because he had to look in her dejected gaze to do it. And because he also knew that *he'd* put that look there.

On the other hand, this suddenly felt like the easiest thing he'd done in his life.

"I came to tell you that I'm the fool. Not you."

"I knew that already."

He couldn't stop the quick grin. This was the Bree he'd driven three hours to find. "And I came to tell you that I shouldn't have been such a jerk that night."

She opened her mouth to speak, but he held up a finger and cut her off.

"You knew that already, too, right?"

She nodded. "I did."

"Then did you know that I was wrong that night?"

"How so?"

"In so many ways." He held out a hand. "Will you put your hand in mine while I count them?"

Her eyebrows pulled together slightly, and he could tell she didn't know if she wanted to touch him or not. If she could trust him. But he kept his hand out anyway. Hopeful. He had a litany of ways to spout off to her, and he needed the strength of hope to get him through.

Finally, she slid her hand over his, the soft pads of her fingers smoothing over his rougher ones, and his heart thumped out a sweet song.

He curled the tips of his fingers around the edges of hers, and he took a half step closer. "I was wrong to try to push you away that night," he started. "To be cold and distant. I was wrong not to see the love you were offering as a gift that should have been received." He stopped to breathe. "I was wrong to think I could maintain distance in order to never experience pain. Wrong to hurt you. And I was wrong to look into your eyes and say words you longed to hear . . . only to then take them back."

He paused, wanting to make sure his meaning sunk in.

Her eyelashes dipped briefly, and her breathing grew more rapid. But her hand stayed in his. "You were wrong a lot," she finally said.

Another smile played at the corners of his lips. "More than I've ever been in my life. But I also figured out a few things thanks to that night. Thanks to you."

She watched him carefully. "And what were those things?"

"I was hoping you'd ask." He took another half step closer, and the toes of his shoes bumped with hers. He could bend his head and kiss her if only he had the courage to do so. "I figured out that I can be scared to care for someone, but still care for them at the same time. That I can fear being hurt yet be okay. I figured out that I can make you cry and that it pains me to do so."

Her eyes narrowed slightly. "Who says you made me cry?"

"Are you saying that you didn't?"

When she only smirked in reply, he went on. "I figured out I can be terrified of losing someone I care about for good. I also figured out that I could visit my past in order to move forward toward my future."

Those words put extra interest in her eyes. "What do you mean by that?"

"I mean that I sought out and found April. I went to see her the other day."

She sucked in a breath. "Is she okay?"

"She's better than okay. It took her almost a year to get fully back on her feet, but she's finishing up medical school now. Unlike me, she's going to be a real doctor someday."

A smile brightened Bree's face. "Good for her."

His throat tightened. "I also figured out that I can love, Bree. And that it's the best feeling in the world. I figured out that I love *you*." His heart pounded hard inside his chest. "And one of the reasons I came here this morning was to tell you that I can't stand the thought of you missing out on today's reveal. You should be there, no matter what you think about me. So, if it takes me skipping it for you to go . . . then that's what I'll do. But just go. *Please.* You deserve this moment."

"I'm already planning to go. I was upstairs packing when you got here." She swallowed, then licked her lips. "And for the record, you *don't* have to skip it."

"Does that mean that you don't hate me?"

"I don't know what it means yet."

He nodded. He knew he'd have to work hard at this. "Then what else can I say to convince you, sweetheart?"

"To convince me of what?"

He couldn't believe she was making him spell it out to her. "To take me back, of course. I was pushing you away that night because you terrified me. I hope you can understand that."

"And what? I don't terrify you anymore?"

He grinned. He loved that she refused to cave easily. He also loved her spirit. "The only thing that terrifies me now is the idea of you saying no to coming back to me. To seeing what we can build together. To staying with me even when I do stupid things —and good Lord, I do fear that I'll do more stupid things."

"I would bet on it."

He tilted his head and looked down at her. "So will you do it? Will you come home to me?"

"I won't be treated like that again, Justin. So callously. Not even by someone I love."

His hand squeezed hers. "And I won't ever treat you like that again. I was a fool. Not just for saying that word to you, but for not realizing how much you mean to me before now. How much I love you. But it became clear this week that if I didn't figure things out, I was going to lose you for good. My best friend. My love. Please tell me that I haven't lost you for good. Please tell me there's still a chance."

She studied him for a moment, and then she glanced out the window gracing the front wall. "What if I slept with Cord?" she asked. "Would that change anything you've said here today?"

Her question made his chest ache. He loved her so much. "No." He shook his head, but it pained him to do so. "It wouldn't change *anything* I've said today. I'd regret my part in pushing you that way, absolutely. But if that's what happened, then that's the reality I'm prepared to live with. I would, however"—he reached behind him and pulled her pink bra from his back pocket—"have to burn this bra if it's the same pink one you wore that night when you were expecting to hook up with him."

She eyed the lace and satin garment in his hand. "It's not the same one."

"So there's another one I need to burn?"

A smile threatened at her lips, and he knew that he definitely saw a softening in her eyes. He might get her back yet. And if he did, he hoped he never did anything to risk losing her again.

"I didn't sleep with Cord, Justin. I've never even kissed him.

He showed up here today about three minutes before you did, and he certainly didn't come to see me."

Justin closed his eyes in relief. And he almost pulled Bree into his arms.

Forcing his eyes open again, he let her see all the anguish of the last week mixed in with the love he'd hold for her forever. And then he took both her hands into his and pulled her flush with him. "Love me, Bree. Be with me. Kick my ass whenever I'm stupid, but be there to climb into my bed every night. Come back to me, Bree. And love me forever."

She didn't hesitate that time. Instead, a smile graced her face, and her eyes shone with love. "Of course I'll come back to you, Justin. This is all I've ever wanted. For you to see that although we're good as friends, we can be unstoppable as lovers."

He kissed her then, not needing to hear anything else but desperately needing to feel her in his arms, and when he finally pulled back, she was still smiling up at him.

"I love you," she said, and he immediately nodded.

"I love you, too. I'll love you forever."

"Let's go home, Justin. I have a party to attend. And guess what? I'm even going to let you drive me to the building this afternoon. But only because I don't want to get the bottom of my gown wet in the snow."

He chuckled, ready to drive her anywhere or nowhere. Whatever she needed, all she'd ever have to do was ask.

After they gathered up her clothes and told her sister goodbye, they both piled into his car with plans to come back and retrieve hers another day. They wanted to spend the drive home together, and he couldn't be more pleased.

As he pulled out and pointed the car down the highway, she asked, "How did you know I was at Erica's? Did my mother cave and tell you, or did she tell your mother and then *your* mother told you?"

He glanced across the seat at her. "Actually, my father got it out of your father."

"Really? I wouldn't have guessed that."

"My father and I had several long chats this week," he explained. "Apparently, we've opened the door to communication. And part of what he communicated was that I was an idiot if I let you slip away."

"Good for him." She plucked the bra out from where he'd stuck it back into his pocket. "So, you travel around with my bra in your pocket now?"

He reached into the glove compartment and pulled out the red one from three years before. "When I'm desperate to show how much I love you, I'll stash your bras wherever needed."

She laughed, and they headed for home.

CHAPTER SIXTEEN

Bree stepped inside the first set of double doors to the office building, Justin by her side, and shrugged out of her white, faux-fur wrap. As she did—*as expected*—Justin's jaw dropped.

"Better than the dress I wore to your office party?" she asked.

"Better than anyone here needs to see."

She laughed, his implied compliment, along with the accompanying one written in the heated glow of his eyes, telling her all she needed to know. The silver sequined trumpet dress with the cinched in waist and the moderately plunging neckline hit exactly the note she'd hoped. Because when one helps to create a masterpiece on a three-story wall, one needed to make sure she didn't get missed.

And she didn't plan on being missed tonight. After all, she did love to party.

"Shall we go in?" she asked.

"Lead the way."

They passed through the second set of doors, and Justin's mother spotted them immediately. She came over with her husband and Bree's parents in tow, and then the six of them headed to the platform that had been added for the evening and took their places beside the mayor and city council. Bree and Justin had been running late. They might have had to stop in a deserted parking lot on the drive home to fully make up after a long, lonely week, and they'd barely made it back in time for her to shower and change. Mrs. Cory had assured them that the unveiling would wait for the star player, though, and now that they were all here, the energy in the room seemed to grow.

The place was packed. Additional decorations had been added since she'd last been inside the building. Mostly fake snow drifts piled along the edges of the room, as well as long, sweeping boughs of flocked garland and hanging red and silver trim. Lights weaved throughout all of it, and spotlights had been installed in the ceiling, pointing toward the wall.

Of course, the mural remained covered at the moment. The scaffolding had been removed, and the work curtain had been replaced with a pleated velvet one. And still hanging from the middle of the room was the largest bundle of mistletoe she'd ever seen. Bree tilted her head back to take in the mistletoe—it was directly above the platform where the group of them stood—and thought about the night of Justin's office party. She wondered if things would have even happened for them if that mistletoe hadn't been there. But then she glanced over at the love shining from Justin's eyes and decided that mistletoe or not, something would have happened to make sure they came together. After all, wasn't that the kind of magic the season brought out?

She smiled at the man she loved, grateful for the opportunities both in her past and in the years to come, and silently promised that wherever those opportunities took her, she would always return home to this.

"Ladies and gentlemen," Mayor Garrett spoke into the microphone, capturing the room's attention. "We want to thank everyone for coming out tonight, and before we do the official unveiling, we'd like to take a moment to properly introduce you to the ladies who've made this masterpiece possible."

About the Author

Photography by Amelia Moore

As a child, Kim Law cultivated a love for chocolate, anything purple, and creative writing. She penned her debut work, "The Gigantic Talking Raisin," in the sixth grade and got hooked on the delights of creating stories. Before settling into the writing life, however, she earned a college degree in mathematics, then worked as a computer programmer while raising her son. Now she's pursuing her lifelong dream of writing romance novels—none of which include talking raisins.

A native of Kentucky, Kim now resides in Middle Tennessee. You can visit Kim at www.KimLaw.com.

Additional comments were shared by the mayor before she brought both Bree and Mrs. Cory to the center of the stage, and after the applause died down, the attendants waiting to drop the curtain were given the nod. A drum roll sounded from speakers, and the gathered group seemed to hold their breaths. And in the next instant, the curtain dropped, and the room remained silent. Even Bree couldn't find words to describe it.

She'd known how to highlight certain aspects to play off the overhead spotlighting, of course, but until just now, she'd not managed to see the entire piece lit up unencumbered. And it was breathtaking. So good, in fact, that the sight brought her to tears.

She'd done that.

And without doubt, she would soon be doing more of it.

The room suddenly exploded with applause, and the next hour and a half was spent with a line of people making their way to Bree. They all congratulated her on a job well done and gushed over her talent, several asking to hire her for rooms in their own homes, and as the line finally began to dwindle, she noticed that her cheeks had started to ache from all the smiling. She didn't mind the ache, though. This was a perfect party.

They'd moved off to the side shortly after the unveiling because it had quickly become clear the platform would be used with regularity for a little under-the-mistletoe kissing. And as the latest well-wisher made their way past Bree, a hand touched her at the small of her back, and she looked up to find Justin.

"I love you," he said.

"I love you, too."

He held up a large cardboard mailer. "I also have something for you."

She brightened. A present? There was a glittery red bow attached to one side of the envelope.

"Yep. Your Christmas present."

"*Oh.*" She gave him a secretive smile and did a little shimmy with her shoulders. She planned to give him his present later tonight—it was the strapless Christmas-themed bra currently in place under the dress she wore—and accepted his gift.

Ripping the perforated strip from one end, she looked at him in question. It looked as if there might be a photo inside. And as she pulled out the contents, she saw that that's exactly what it was. A 10x14 glossy of her and Justin kissing under the mistletoe that night at his party. And as she gazed down upon it, she realized that what she saw captured in the moment was two people who'd been utterly smitten. Who'd had no clue in that moment that the rest of the world even existed.

"That's when I fell in love with you," Justin told her. "I didn't know it at the time, and it took you leaving for me to start to get a clue, but this moment set the course for the rest of my life."

She kissed him then, not caring who might be watching or what they might be thinking, and as she pulled back, remaining wrapped tightly in his arms, she turned her head and tucked it into his chest. Currently standing underneath the mistletoe in the middle of the room, was a girl appearing to be in her mid-teens, kissing a boy who seemed as quiet and stay-in-the-shadows as Justin once had.

"First love," she murmured. "I wonder who they are."

Justin followed her line of sight, and then she felt a satisfied sigh ripple through him. "That's Jamie," he told her. "She's one of my patients, and the boy's father works in this building. The boy has been avoiding her anytime they'd both been near that mistletoe together, but that hasn't deterred Jamie. She's been planning this moment for weeks."

Bree sighed, as well. "I'm glad she finally caught her man."

"And I'm glad you did."

ACKNOWLEDGMENTS

Huge thanks go out to some of my readers for quick turnaround times to help me get this book polished and ready to go. Thank you to Cindy Tew, Deb Fernow, Kay Hutcherson, Staci Forsythe, and Bette Hansen. You ladies rock in all sorts of ways!

Made in the USA
Monee, IL
05 December 2021